Joint Custody

Joint Custody

Lauren Baratz-Logsted
and
Jackie Logsted

JOVE
New York

A JOVE BOOK
Published by Berkley
An imprint of Penguin Random House LLC
penguinrandomhouse.com

Library of Congress Cataloging-in-Publication Data

Names: Baratz-Logsted, Lauren, author. | Logsted, Jackie, author.
Title: Joint custody / Lauren Baratz-Logsted and Jackie Logsted.
Description: First edition. | New York : Jove, 2021.
Identifiers: LCCN 2020025903 (print) | LCCN 2020025904 (ebook) |
ISBN 9780593199589 (trade paperback) | ISBN 9780593199596 (ebook)
Subjects: GSAFD: Humorous fiction. | Love stories.
Classification: LCC PS3602.A754 J65 2021 (print) | LCC PS3602.A754 (ebook) |
DDC 813/.6—dc23
LC record available at https://lccn.loc.gov/2020025903
LC ebook record available at https://lccn.loc.gov/2020025904

First Edition: January 2021

Printed in the United States of America
1   3   5   7   9   10   8   6   4   2

Cover images: Dog by TimmerTammer / Shutterstock;
Chocolates by Arina P. Habich / Shutterstock
Cover design by Sarah Oberrender
Book design by Nancy Resnick
Title page image by Evgeniya Chertova / Shutterstock

For Greg Logsted. There is no us without you.

Chapter One

It all started with the chocolates.

Ah, who am I kidding?

It all nearly ended with the chocolates too.

It was the best idea I ever had. It was the worst idea I ever had. It was an idea that could save them. It was an idea that could kill me. Did you see that? I just riffed on Dickens there. Not as good, I know, but bear with me.

The day was cold and brisk. I knew, because I'd been out already once for my morning walk, up and down the tree-lined sidewalk of the street outside our Brooklyn brownstone. But it was also bright and sunny, the golden rays acting like a beacon as they shone across the dining room table, spotlighting the heart-shaped box wrapped in red cellophane. I'd seen boxes like that before and knew what they contained.

I needed to get to that box.

First, I hopped up onto the wooden chair. And from there, I hopped up onto the round table, shoving a marked-up manuscript out of the way to get closer to my goal. The Man is a writer, and there are books everywhere in this place—controlled chaos.

Now I was face-to-face with the box. If I had to guess, I'd say it weighed a pound. Also, it said it right there on the front: lb looks like *el-bee*, but it means one pound, right?

OK, I know what you're thinking right around now. You're thinking, *The dog can read?* Which is soon naturally followed by, *Preposterous!*

Well, think on this: consider the infinite monkey theorem. Come on, you know what that is, right? It's the theorem that states that "a monkey hitting keys at random on a typewriter keyboard for an infinite amount of time will almost surely type a given text, such as the complete works of William Shakespeare."

Of course, that's just a metaphor. But the way people bandy it around, you'd think chimps were pumping out five-act plays in iambic pentameter on a regular basis. If people will believe such a positive thing about chimps, when everyone knows that if you try to make a pet out of a chimp it might one day kill you, then it's really not such a great leap to think that a dog could learn how to read. Particularly a smart dog who's grown up in a home crammed full of great books.

And hey, it's not like I claimed I could write a book.

I'm no chimp.

But I might have been a chump. Because as I stared at that sealed red cellophane, contemplating my suicide mission, I had to ask the question: Could I really bring myself to do this?

Well, I thought, at the very least, I could remove the cellophane. And then, you know, make my decision once the box was open. I'd no doubt get in trouble merely for marring the packaging, but it was a risk I was willing to take.

And honestly, just getting that wrapping off presented its own joys—the crinkling noises; the mere act of rebellion itself—as well as its inherent risks. At one point, I heard sounds coming from the bedroom. Immediately, I stopped what I was doing, ears going straight up. These days, The Man often goes back to bed after our morning walk—he suffers from a mild, sometimes more than mild, depression—which is why I'd timed this the way I had. If he was awake, I could never get away with this. But soon the noise from the bedroom ceased, and after waiting one long minute more just to be sure, I resumed my efforts.

Not so easy, given I'd just had my nails clipped the night before. How I hate it when my nails have just been clipped. Nothing feels right, I tell you.

But eventually, the heart-shaped box was free of its cellophane wrapping. The box itself was also red, and now I eyed it warily.

Again, the question arose in me: Could I really bring myself to do this?

Well, I thought, at least I could take the lid off. Then I'd worry about it.

The lid wasn't nearly as challenging as the cellophane had been. Just a firm nudge of my snout and I'd popped that baby right off.

And then, the question one final time, as I faced the array of chocolates:

Could I really bring myself to do this?

Of course I could.

I'd brought them together once. I would bring them together again, no matter what it took, even if it killed me.

Doing something that could bring about your own death when you don't really want to die—it's not the easiest thing to do.

But then I thought: *It's all about the happy ending* . . .

And as the chorus from the Bruno Mars song "Grenade" began running on a loop in my brain—y'know, jumping in front of trains, catching grenades; I told myself it was all just like playing fetch—I dived in.

I nosed around the contents for a time, taking in the scent that was both beautiful and treacherous. But I must admit, after the first taste of chocolate and then maybe the second, I forgot the risks. Because . . .

Ohmygod . . . it tasted *SO. GOOD.*

That taste was so good, and I wanted it to go on and on, forever and ever, so I just kept eating it and eating it until . . .

Holy crap. How did that box get so empty?

Well, except for all the little brown wrappers. There were wrappers *everywhere*.

But the chocolate? Every last bit—the milk chocolates and the dark chocolates, the chocolates with cream inside and the chocolates with caramel and the chocolates with nuts and even the chocolates with that crappy Roman nougat stuff (I mean, what is that crap even made out of?). All of it gone. All of it now inside me.

I'm guessing it was the sound of me running around the place like a maniac that finally woke The Man. That and the smell of the vomit. Maybe the diarrhea.

"Gatz! Oh my god, Gatz!"

In my near-comatose state, at the sound of The Man's panicked voice, I tilted my eyes over to see The Man standing in the doorway to the bedroom, his depression bathrobe hanging open over his T-shirt and jeans, Mets ball cap on backward per the usual, feet bare.

By the way, I was named after that guy who dies in the swimming pool. Don't judge. It's his favorite book. Hers too.

OK, so maybe this isn't the right time for a primer on my name.

"Gatz! What did you do?" The Man cried, rushing over to where I lay on the floor in my filth and my empty wrappers. It might sound like he was mad at me, but he wasn't. There was real anguish in his voice, and I felt so bad for putting it there. I hated hurting The Man, but I had to do it. It was for his own good. Again, hers too.

"You know better!" The Man said as he fumbled for his cell phone.

Well, of *course* I know better, you nitwit. Hey, it's part of my master plan!

"Just hang in there, Gatz," The Man said, patting me reassuringly as he held the phone to his ear, waiting for someone to pick up.

Yes! I thought. *He's calling The Woman—score! Finally! I knew he'd call her, I knew it, I knew it, I—*

Only it turned out he wasn't calling The Woman after all, which I could tell by the way he spoke to whoever was on the other end of the line.

"Black-and-white border collie," he said.

"Three years old," he said.

"Twenty-two pounds," he said.

See, that's when I knew he hadn't called The Woman, because he wouldn't need to tell her all that stuff about me. The Woman already knew all that stuff about me.

About those twenty-two pounds: I'm on the low range of weight for my breed, but what can I say? I may be tiny in size, but I'm mighty in how I love. Apart from the gender, what Helena said of Hermia in *A Midsummer Night's Dream* is true of me too: "Though she be but little, she is fierce."

Realizing that The Man was not talking to The Woman, but rather, what sounded like it was probably some animal hospital, I promptly puked again.

The Man scratched the side of his face with the fingers on the hand that was holding the phone to his ear, as he continued to soothe me with the other hand and said, "I don't know. It looks like the whole box? I don't remember what size I bought. Maybe a pound?"

I didn't know either anymore. By that point I'd started to tremble so bad, my heart pounding harder than it ever had in my whole life, it was pretty difficult for me to focus.

"Yes, I'll bring him right in." The Man's voice came to me through my delirium. "And the box too."

A minute later, I felt a blanket being wrapped around my trembling body and The Man lifting me up into his arms, filth and all.

If that's not love, I don't know what is.

Then he hurried down the stairs with the empty box of chocolates and me, out the door and into the car, where he buckled me into the passenger seat beside him—safety first.

As we peeled away from the curb, I heard him pushing buttons on his phone again. If I could have, I would have yelled, *SAFETY FIRST!* at him, because every idiot knows you're not supposed to use a hand-held device while driving, but then I realized that finally—finally!—he was calling The Woman, and I no longer cared about safety. Not at all.

As they spoke, I pictured The Woman in the Manhattan office of the publishing company where she's an editor: tall, dark skin, beautiful, elegant hairstyle and with a charming slight gap between her front teeth, slight British accent when she speaks. And the office? It's as tidy as a book editor's can be, books coming out an equal distance to the millimeter on the shelves lining the room. For her, the alphabet will always be an exact science, *not* an approximate art. I know all this because when others at the company bring their human offspring in for Take Your Child to Work Day, she always brings me. And hey, I'm always a big hit.

Remembering safety, The Man activated the speaker function, setting the phone in the device holder so he could keep both hands on the wheel.

"What's going on?" The Woman said.

"It's Gatz," The Man said. "He ate chocolate."

"*What? How much?*"

"Um . . . a lot."

"How much is a lot?" I could hear her sense of urgency rising. "Is a lot like a couple of bites of a bar or a whole chocolate Santa?"

"It's February."

Even in my haze, I knew what The Man was getting at with that ominous "February." But thankfully, she didn't.

"I know it's February," she said. "How much candy did he eat?"

"A box full."

"Oh geez."

Oh yes!

"I just thought you'd want to know," The Man said.

"Thank you, I'm so glad you called."

She's so glad!

"In case you want to meet us there," The Man said.

In case she wants to meet us there!

"I know you love him too," The Man said. "That's why I called."

That's why he called!

"I'm on my way," The Woman said.

She's on her way! She's on her way! She's on her—

And then he hung up, and soon we were at our destination, not caring that double-parking might earn us a ticket or a tow, the passenger door opening, him scooping me into his arms again, filth and all plus the empty box, and he was hustling me inside, his bare feet wet and raw from the slushy sidewalks because he'd neglected to throw on shoes in his rush to save my life.

Some might think it unrealistic, that a person wouldn't put on shoes in the middle of winter. But I say: Have you ever needed to save somebody's life before? When every second is critical, life or death? Would you really stop and say, "Hey, pal, can you die a little slower here—I need to find my galoshes"? If I'd "Grenade" myself for The Man, unlike in the song, The Man would totally do the same for me.

We were met at the door by a vet in a white coat. She was pretty enough—think Amy Klobuchar in a lab coat—but not like The Woman. Still, I appreciated how calm she was—The Man was such a wreck at this point, he was starting to make me nervous—and her hands felt so cool on my forehead.

Then she took the box from him.

"Two pounds?" she said. "I thought on the phone you said it was one pound."

Wait. What?

Ah, crap. When I'd seen the "lb" on the front of the box, I thought it meant it was just one pound. I hadn't paid attention to any number that might have been before it. Apparently, The Man hadn't either, and he's the one who bought the thing. What can I say, neither of us has ever been good with numbers. A dog might write you a book, but he's never going to do your taxes.

"Let's get him inside," she said briskly.

As they rushed me down the hallway to an examination room, she didn't have to add that two pounds could kill me.

We all knew that.

As much as I had wanted and intended to do this, I hadn't actually planned on *dying*.

That's when my life flashed before my eyes. And as it did, I wondered who would voice me in the movie version of my life. I kind of hoped it would be Paul Giamatti, but somehow, I suspected that Hollywood would go for Brad Pitt. That could be OK too, I guess. Or maybe they'd try to make me British, like The Woman, and go with Idris Elba.

And now the vet was working on me, inducing vomiting—not something I was a particular fan of. And hey, hadn't I done this enough already? Then she was giving me activated charcoal to absorb the remaining toxins and hooking up an IV to get fluids into me. All the while, she was explaining how such a large quantity of chocolate presented a grave danger to one as small as I, and how the dark chocolates were more dangerous than the milk chocolates and how white chocolates would have been the best of all, and how it was really the theobromine that posed the biggest danger.

I felt like telling her, *Yeah, yeah, I know all this already, lady, from that one time I ate chocolate when I was still a puppy.*

Hey, I was just a puppy then. I didn't know any better. Anyway, it was just a few Hershey's Kisses.

Well, maybe more than a few.

Don't judge.

But past mistakes no longer mattered, even present mistakes didn't matter, because right then I heard a new voice penetrating my fog of pain and discomfort.

"Gatz!" the new voice cried.

It was The Woman.

She must've dropped everything and hopped in a cab the minute she got off the phone with The Man. *God*, I loved this woman.

And then she was dropping her things inside the doorway, barely giving The Man a once-over, her eyes finally noticing those wet, raw feet.

"Your poor feet!" she exclaimed in sympathy.

See? She still cares about him! I thought.

But The Man just shook his head—like his own discomfort didn't matter, not one bit—and then she was hurrying to my side, across from The Man on the other side. Soon, each was holding one of my paws. This couldn't have been going any better if I'd planned it. OK, I *had* planned it. But can you blame me? Anyone seeing these two together had to see what I saw: they were made for each other.

If I hadn't felt so lousy, I would have been ecstatic.

Across the examination table, their eyes met.

This was it, the moment we'd all been waiting for . . .

"Hi," The Man said.

"Hi," The Woman said.

Yes! They were saying hi to each other!

"Gatz," she said, "how could you do this? You know better."

Me knowing better seemed to be the recurrent theme of the day.

Yeah, I thought, feeling myself go all hangdog, for want of a better way to put it, *I do. But someone had to do something to bring you two crazy kids back together.*

And they really were together, because The Man reached an open hand across my body, and The Woman took it, practically causing me to squeal with uncomplicated joy, and The Man said, "It's going to be OK. It has to be."

In that moment, I tell you, everything was right in my world.

Even if I died today, it would be OK.

The Man smiled at The Woman warmly, and she smiled back: bliss, at least for me.

"How did this happen?" The Woman said. And again the refrain: "Gatz knows better."

Then she looked around the room, and something made the soft expression go out of her eyes. Instead, her eyes hardened as the hand holding my paw stiffened.

"Valentine's Day chocolates?" she asked The Man, sounding wounded. "Who were those for?"

Ah, crap.

That's not how this was supposed to go.

Chapter Two

Three years earlier...

It was love at first sight. The minute he walked into the animal rescue shelter, I knew he was the one.

All I knew about my humble origins was that I'd been abandoned at the shelter with my three littermates, none of whom I ever saw again. One shelter worker had said to the other, "I'll never understand how people who live in the city can *not* fix their dogs"; to which her coworker had replied, "Well, if they all did, we'd be out of a job." And that was that.

It was a day like any other day in the land of desperation, the smell of group urine high in the air. There were all kinds of dogs with snouts pressed up against the front of their cages for as far as my eye could see, all eagerly barking at the potential owners walking by. They all wanted to be adopted by someone, *anyone*.

Even if it was love at first sight, it's not like I didn't have other offers.

Many had tried to adopt me, but I'd held out waiting for the real thing to come along.

It wasn't always easy, the waiting. In fact, it was exactly as hard as Tom Petty said it was. Sure, I'd chase my tail until I was dizzy, I'd pounce on random shadows or rays of light, I'd eat literally anything I found on the floor—once I ate a button, *not* something I'd recommend. In fact, I engaged in all manner of puppy self-entertainment.

But still, the waiting was hard. No one likes to be kept in a cage. Even if it's pretty much all you've ever known, you still know it's no way to live.

Big dogs, small dogs, deranged dogs, cute dogs: no matter what their strengths, or lack thereof, no one was paying any attention to them. Because none of the customers stopped until they got to my cage.

The ones who tried to adopt me may have seemed infinite in their variety, but in the end it all boiled down to the same problem.

Take the first couple who tried: two men in their twenties, expensive but stylish suits, identical pairs of Warby Parker in place. We'll call them Corporate Man #1 and Corporate Man #2, since the only real thing distinguishing them for our purposes is that #2's wedding ring was far more ornate than #1's.

They squatted in front of my cage, careful not to let the knees of their suits come in contact with the questionable concrete floor, oohing and aahing over how cute I was.

Trust me, this was nothing I hadn't heard before.

"I'm telling you, babe," #1 said, "this is the dog."

"Seriously," #2 said. "Is there a cuter dog in all of Brooklyn?"

These two might've thought I'd make the perfect addition to their family, but I knew their kind. I'd already seen them, many times before: busy-busy professionals who'd leave me to my own devices for ridiculously long stretches of the day and night. Why'd they even want a dog in the first place? With these two, I'd be home alone all the time, just another trophy dog. The way I figured it, if these two wanted a pet so badly, they could get a turtle. Or a goldfish. I didn't really care. The only thing I did care about was that there was no way I was going to let these two adopt *this guy*.

And to make sure that would never, ever happen, I began barking violently, transforming myself into a holy terror, embarking on a string of barks that would've made Cujo look like Lassie. It wasn't long before the two men were backing away, horrified.

"Fine, buddy," #2 said, "we'll look somewhere else. Jesus . . ."

Yeah, that's right, I thought, barking hard at their retreating backs to ensure they didn't even think of changing their minds again, *go look somewhere else. And while you're looking somewhere else, you might rethink your policy of addressing living beings you've barely met as "buddy"!*

I could hear the other dogs squealing in my general direction, desperately hoping to draw some of the attention away from me. Trust me, I wouldn't have minded if they'd succeeded. But alas, no.

Next up was your classic nuclear family: bored father, uptight wife, a boy and a girl—about two years apart—in soccer uniforms, fighting over dad's cell phone. I figured if the parents could've found a way to have 2.4 kids, instead of two, they'd have gone for it to achieve perfect nuclear family status.

The uptight wife gazed in at me, her aspirations clear in her eyes.

"Oh my god, he's so cute!" she squealed. "Charles, take a look."

It was apparent that Bored Husband hadn't been asked for his opinion on anything in a very long time, but when he glanced over at me, I could see that he was struck by my beauty. For the first time in probably forever for him, he didn't look bored.

"Oh, wow, honey," he gushed, "he is *so* cute!" And then he focused his attention more closely on me. "You are so cute! Yes, you are!"

Oh brother.

The kids, no doubt shocked to hear their dad's voice shoot up to such a high octave, looked over to see what all the fuss was about. Instantly spellbound, their dad's cell phone forgotten for the time being, they joined their parents in front of my cage.

The boy and girl spoke rapidly and simultaneously, but it's impossible for me to re-create that without making myself mentally dizzy and physically nauseous, so I'll simply recount them one after another.

From the little boy: "Oh my god, he's so cute! He is the cutest dog! Can we get him, can we get him? Now, now, now, now, now, now, now, now, now, now, now—"

And from the little girl: "He's so cute, so perfectly cute! All I want to do is put him in a mini soccer uniform and show all my friends so that everyone else can see how perfectly cute—"

Yawn. I'd been over these 2.4-wannabes since the moment they approached my cage.

Hey, I like a compliment as much as the next dog, but come up with something original at least; maybe try a different adjective. I mean, come on, I already knew I was cute.

Out of patience, I let loose another series of demonic barks. Good-bye, Snoopy; and hello, Cerberus, aka the hound of Hades, aka the multiheaded devil dog who guards the gates to the Underworld and prevents the dead from leaving.

Who's cute now? I thought.

Finally getting the message that I was no docile lapdog, Nuclear Family's collective eyes went wide and then they bolted away from my cage. Now, they couldn't get away from me fast enough, but before they could entirely escape the building, I saw a harried shelter worker rush after them, desperately pleading, "He's not really like this! He's usually so nice!"

But it was too late. They were gone, and good riddance.

The shelter worker made her way back to my cage and squatted down before me.

"Why are you being like this, boy?" she asked in a puzzled voice. "I know you're a good dog; I mean, a *really* good dog."

Well, of *course* I'm a good dog. Duh.

The shelter worked added, more puzzled yet, "Don't you want to get adopted? Don't you want to go to a good home?"

Yes and yes, the operative word here being "good."

No way was I going to let myself be adopted by an inferior grouping of humans.

Shrugging, the shelter worker scratched my belly until she got called away to attend to some minor emergency. Grinning and satisfied with how I was handling my day so far, I curled up for a nap.

I don't know how much time had passed, but I was in that half-waking/half-sleeping twilight zone—you know the one I'm talking about, the one where you see images of yourself living your best life and it feels so real, you're sure it just has to be really happening—when I heard a *click* that sounded completely wrong somehow, and instantly, I was fully awake.

Where the hell did she come from? was all I could think.

Because there before me—*In. My. Cage.*—was a little girl who might just as well have had a sign over her head announcing her name as being Hell on Earth.

Covered in glitter, pigtailed, retainer clad—I swear she was even drooling. Can you imagine anything worse to wake up to? And did I mention the part about her being In. My. Cage???

But how did she . . .

Why would she . . .

I opened my mouth to bark, hoping to draw the attention of the kindly shelter worker so she could fix this egregious breach of shelter etiquette. But for once, all that came out was a quiet whimper. Hell on Earth was so hellish, she'd scared the bark right out of me.

And you know what was worse?

When she put her face close to mine and said, "Oh, she's so cute!"

She? *She?* Could Hell on Earth not see the evidence of maleness dangling proudly between my legs?

What an insult!

Sure, I'd been fixed—I remember right before they performed the procedure, one shelter worker telling me that it wouldn't hurt, that it was for my own good, that there were already too many unwanted puppies (a sad thought, that) in the world—but hey, I still had The Main Event!

I scurried backward, away from this monstrosity of a human child. But before I could get out even another pathetic little whimper, Hell on Earth had swiftly grabbed me by the fur, dragging me outside my cage. Normally, I'd love to get outside my cage. But not under these circumstances.

Then she proceeded to lift me in the air, hoisting me upward in her odious hands in the most undignified way possible—on my back, clutched to her chest like I was some kind of . . . *cat*. Then she pushed her face right into mine as she intoned the dreaded words:

"You're mine now, doggo."

Did I mention that she held me *like a cat*?

'Nuff said.

If she was going to push her face into mine, then I was going to push mine right back into hers, forehead drilling into forehead. Then, finally finding my voice again, I let out my most sadistic, wolverine barks yet. This time, I was Cujo *and* Cerberus, combined.

If I must say so myself, I was glorious.

With a shriek, Hell on Earth practically threw me to the ground, patently disgusted with my behavior.

Honey, I thought, *that makes two of us*.

And, as she walked away, I further thought, *Get the Pomeranian—you two deserve each other. Plus, she's actually a she!*

But pleased with my own behavior as I was, as I brushed myself off and slunk back into my cage, I have to admit, I was starting to feel defeated.

Was I never going to find a right-for-me forever home?

I'm not sure how much time had passed, but I was slumped over, head on my paws, feeling dejected about my depressing slew of options. It was in this sorry state that I pressed my jowls against the mesh of the cage, my eyes tracking down the long concrete corridor to the door at the far end. What I saw there intrigued me, instantly perking up my emotional state.

He walked in . . .

At the door was The Man, my first-ever sighting of him. There he stood, in all his disheveled glory, looking around at the shelter like he wasn't sure if he'd come to the right place or if he should even be there at all.

But if he was uncertain, for the first time in my life, I was completely certain.

And who wouldn't be?

Because as he stood there at the end of the corridor, it was as though a halo of yellow light shot rays outward from around his head—you know, like you see in portraits of Jesus. OK, so maybe it was the fluorescent bulb overhead creating the effect, but I don't think so. After all, I hadn't seen this happen to anyone else who walked through the doors.

His eyes traveled around the space, and I could see disappointment in them, mirroring the disappointment I'd felt earlier. He began to turn away, and I realized he hadn't seen me yet. Desperate for him not to go, I pressed my snout farther into the wire mesh and commenced to barking, only this time, these weren't the menacing barks I'd let out earlier; these were friendly, come-hither, enticing, I-want-you-to-fall-in-love-with-me-like-I'm-falling-in-love-with-you barks.

He turned back, his eyes locking onto mine. No longer did he look disappointed. On the contrary, I could practically hear the music swelling around us as we connected. As if enchanted, he moved past the line of barking dogs and straight up to my cage. But when he got there, rather than coming on too strong, like everyone else did, when he crouched down, he maintained a respectful distance between us.

"Hey, buddy," he started.

And for the first time in my life, I didn't mind someone calling me "buddy." Not when he said it.

"It's so nice to meet you," he went on. "I'm—"

I must confess, I was so besotted at this point that I didn't catch his name or anything else he said immediately. I was so entranced that the specifics of the sounds he was making didn't register in my ears, and from this moment onward, he would forever be The Man to me. There might be other men on the planet—billions of them, in fact—but there would only ever be one The Man.

When I calmed down enough to register specific words again, I tuned in just in time to hear him say, "Gosh, I'd sure love to have you come home with me, but of course, it's entirely up to you."

I wagged my tail a bit.

Yes! He cared about my opinion of things!

"Let me tell you a little bit about myself," The Man said, "to maybe help you decide. So, um, I'm a writer. That means I'm home a lot . . ."

I wagged my tail harder.

Yes! YES!

"Actually, I don't like going out," The Man went on, "so really, I'm home almost all the time . . ."

I wagged my tail so hard it was like a wagging blur.

YES! YES! I'd hardly ever be alone!

"But I'll give you your space too," he said. "I do know how important that is . . ."

He was nice but not too nice, intelligent but not too intelligent—what more could I want? Plus, he smelled like all the best foods.

"I understand if you want to go in a different direction," The Man said. "I'm sure you've had a lot of other offers."

Well, sure. But not like this.

"But if you decide—"

I couldn't stand it anymore. If that Hell on Earth nightmare had figured out how to unlock the cage, I figured it couldn't be too hard. So that's exactly what I did, bursting out of the cage and jumping straight into The Man's open arms, covering his face in loving licks.

"Well, OK then!" The Man said. "I guess that settles that!"

And then he looked down at me, with all the love in the world.

Chapter Three

Still three years ago...

The paperwork took a long time, but then, before I knew it, we were out of that hellhole. OK, so maybe it wasn't a hellhole at all, and the shelter workers were all very nice to me, but still . . .

I was on my way to my forever home!

But first, we had to get there.

And that was OK too. Picture us: just a couple of cool dudes, walking down the street together side by side, hanging out, not a care to trouble us. Everything was right with our world.

I did lunge at car horns, I tried to eat things off the ground until The Man gently stopped me, I sniffed at dog butts whenever they passed going the other way—but hey, the outside world was all so new to me.

Of course, we'd have made quicker progress toward our goal were it not for all the people who tried to stop us. People say New Yorkers are aloof—cold, even—but that's never been my experience. So many of them tried to stop The Man, commenting on how cute I was. Even though that's not my favorite compliment, which has been previously stated, I do enjoy being adored. Inevitably, though, the people would want to pet me, to which The Man said no. I appreciated that about him, since just because I like being adored, it doesn't mean I want strangers' hands all over me twenty-four seven. Would you?

But then, *she* came into view.

Actually, we heard her before we saw her.

"What a handsome dog! Would it be all right if I pet him?"

That voice. Slightly British. Sophisticated. Rich. It sounded like she was singing the words rather than speaking them.

We looked to the source of that voice—oh, that face! Kind, intelligent, beautiful—she was *perfect*. I must admit, we were both so stunned by her, we froze where we stood. From my position looking up at her, her head seemed to be resting directly in front of the sun, which created a halo effect around her not dissimilar to the one around The Man when I'd first laid eyes on him.

The Man and I reacted simultaneously, me barking my approval of *Oh, my, god* at the exact moment he spoke the words aloud: "Oh, my, god."

You'd have said it too. There was just something about her.

"What?" she said, clearly puzzled by us.

Immediately, we shook ourselves out of our joint trance.

"I'm sorry," The Man said awkwardly. "Ah, *yes*, yes, you may."

She smiled warmly at him then, charmed by his boyish awkwardness, before comfortably kneeling in her pencil skirt to greet me. Normally preferring to get to know someone first before responding, instead I instantly greeted her with love and licks, collapsing onto my back, a clear invitation to rub my belly, which caused her to laugh delightedly. In that moment, I think she was even more charmed by me than she was by The Man. And that laugh, such a beautiful sound—I could've listened to her laugh all day long. And that accent!

"Your accent," The Man said, proving we were on the same page, "it's lovely. If you don't mind me asking . . ."

"London," she said, "but we moved here when I was small. Funny thing, I kept the accent but my brothers didn't."

"Oh. Like Henry Kissinger."

"Pardon?"

"Henry Kissinger was Nixon's secretary of state."

"Yes, I did know that. But what does Henry Kissinger have to do with me? Are you saying we sound alike, because I don't think—"

"NO! Oh gosh, no. All I meant was that Henry Kissinger has a brother, but while Henry kept the accent, his brother didn't."

"That seems like a very odd factoid to have at your disposal."

"I am odd." He shrugged. "And I like factoids."

"He sure is handsome," she said, once again using the appropriate adjective for me. "What's his name?"

"His name?" The Man said.

"Yes—he does have one, right?"

The Man knelt down beside her so that now they were both petting me. Ah, heaven.

"We actually just left the rescue shelter," The Man said. "I guess I didn't think that . . . It feels weird to randomly name him, you know? As if I *own* him or something . . ."

I stared at The Man in awe. *Oh, you perfect human, you,* I thought.

"I understand what you're saying," she said. "I had a friend who didn't name either of her kids for the first two weeks of their lives because everything she could come up with just felt like a placeholder—settling, you know?—and she wanted to wait until she came up with the right name. Still, you'll need something to call him, and you can't very well just call him Handsome for the rest of his life, can you?"

Lady, if you're doing the calling, Handsome it is!

"I don't know," The Man said. "It's like with Prince Charming. I always felt like, shouldn't the guy have a real name? Joe, maybe? I'm pretty sure the king and queen's last name wasn't Charming."

"No, I don't suspect it was."

She looked at me, clearly enchanted with what she was seeing.

"You know," she said slowly, like an idea was dawning on her. "I think he looks like a Gatz."

"Gatz?" The Man echoed, as he looked me over, considering.

"Gatz," she said, like the reference should be obvious, but not in an insulting way. "Like in *The Great Gatsby*. It's my favorite book."

For whatever reason, The Man was so bowled over by this revelation, he fell back a bit, practically falling despite his sensible shoes.

"It . . . It is?" he said, awed.

She looked over at him, nodding.

At last, The Man burst out with what he could obviously no longer contain: "It's my favorite book too!"

In that moment, I realized she was The Woman—who else could she be?—and I think he also realized it then.

The Woman looked at him more closely, taking all of him in, then she smiled widely.

And that, that was love at first sight too.

Chapter Four

A little less than three years ago...

That first day we met on the street, before we headed off home and she headed wherever she was going, The Woman offered to give The Man her contact info. Trading contact info—I guess it's just something humans do.

He'd seemed perplexed by the idea, causing me to bark at him forcefully like, *Dude, don't be an idiot! She wants to keep in touch! In a city of eight million souls, how are we going to find her again if we don't have her contact info?*

"It's just that," The Woman had explained, for the first time sounding awkward herself, "I only thought: Maybe at some point you'll need someone to watch Gatz? Although, I suppose you've probably got loads of friends who can do that for you . . ."

I remembered what he'd said back at the shelter, about how he mostly stayed at home, about how he didn't really *like* to go out, and I thought: *Have you really looked at this guy? When it comes to friends, I'm pretty sure I'm it!*

Which would've been fine with me—it would've been fine with me for it to just be me and The Man forever and ever . . . until I saw *her.* And now, having seen her, we couldn't let her get away!

So when The Man still hesitated—which was just him being his usual awkward self, I think; you could tell he liked her—I gave him a louder bark, causing him to finally accept her contact info.

Geez, already I was beginning to see that, without me, this guy would probably do all kinds of things wrong.

Like wait too long to call her.

But finally, as luck would have it, a radio station he had on did a retrospective of telephone-related songs. He kept trying to turn the knob to something else, but every time he did, I just nudged it back, meaning I had to listen to Electric Light Orchestra's "Telephone Line," Toto's "Hold the Line," and "Hot Line to Heaven" by Bananarama. Honestly, I thought Blondie's "Call Me" was going to kill me because the radio station played the Alvin and the Chipmunks version and I felt myself getting dizzy from all those high-pitched chipmunk voices. Ooh, vertigo. But then Lionel Richie's "Hello" came on—such a soulful song—and that finally did the trick.

He called and asked her out, she said yes, and they agreed to have dinner.

The Man had selected Nick's as their destination, a local Italian joint with classic red-and-white-checked tablecloths with empty Chianti bottles functioning as candlesticks on the table, multiple colors from previous candles dripping down the sides of the bottles.

Most people wouldn't pick Nick's for a first date, not if they were trying to impress the other person, since it's not very impressive on the surface. Tourists don't go there, millionaires and oligarchs certainly don't go there, and Zagat doesn't even know it exists. But for fifty-seven years they've been plating decent chicken Parm, and if, to a person who didn't know better, it might seem like The Man was just phoning it in, I knew better. I knew that if he wasn't ordering takeout, he was trying.

And the main reason The Man had chosen Nick's? Nick's is as dog-friendly of a restaurant as you'll ever hope to find, and there was no way he could do this without me. From the first moment of their relationship, I was the catalyst, I was the glue.

After making sure the bandanna he'd placed around my neck was tied at a jaunty angle, The Man had similarly taken extra pains with his own personal appearance. Again, others might not see it that way. But I knew: ball cap with no stains on it and for once not on backward; the button-down shirt he had on open over his T-shirt and jeans similarly without stains—The Man had gone all out.

I could only hope, as we headed out the door for the night, that she'd see it that way too. Anyone else might say he looked schlubby, but I thought he looked like a prince.

As for her, what can I say? When we arrived, she was already seated at a table—we'd been five minutes late because he'd agonized for so long about *which* Mets ball cap to wear—and she looked, if anything, even more stunning than she had the first time we'd seen her. She was in professional attire once again, having come straight from the office, but she had a shade of lipstick on that screamed "Evening!" and, anyway, she would've still looked impressive if she were wearing a potato sack.

The Woman stood from her chair as we came toward her, and when we arrived at the table, The Man went into a mild panic: *Do I pull out her chair? Don't I? But wait, she's already been seated, so what do I do???* Sometimes it's way too easy to read what's going on in that overthink-it brain of his. Writers, man.

Thankfully, The Woman didn't appear to notice his extended internal turmoil as he went back and forth on what to do, although you'd have to forgive her if she did wonder why the heck we were all just standing there for so long.

When she finally sat down herself, The Man realized he'd missed his moment. To cover up for any etiquette faux pas he might have committed, he cleared his throat with pseudo self-confidence as he took his own seat across from her.

And to help him cover up, I performed the collapse-on-my-back maneuver, charmingly baring my belly for her to rub if she so desired. If I could've, *I'd* have pulled her chair out earlier, but sometimes you've just gotta go with what you've got.

"I love that you brought Gatz with you!" She clasped her hands with joy before bending down from her seat to give my exposed belly a healthy scratch.

The Man cleared his throat awkwardly before responding, "Um, yes, it's why I chose Nick's. They're dog-friendly."

Dude! I thought. *Way to state the obvious! The sign WE ARE DOG-FRIENDLY in the window is bigger than the sign saying Nick's!*

"Yes." She laughed with a laugh that was not at all judgy. "I did see the sign in the window announcing that fact."

Thankfully, it was time to look at the menus.

A quick perusal of the menu yielded an order of chicken Parm and bottled beer for him, while she ordered the fettuccine carbonara, proving there wasn't a food group on the planet that she had anything against, and the house red.

Me, I got the pasta with melted butter and cheese. It's not actually on the menu, but those of us in the know are aware that the kitchen is always happy to oblige. Sometimes I eat like a child, but I'm not at all ashamed of that fact.

Orders successfully placed, The Man relapsed into a brief period of awkwardness, before jump-starting himself with the tried-and-true:

"I'm so glad you said yes to coming out with me tonight."

"I'm so glad you asked me," she replied.

See? I'd have reassured him as the waiter delivered their drinks order, returning a short time later to place a bowl of water on the floor for me. *This isn't so hard! Now, quick, say something else before you lose your momentum.*

"Well, it's the least I could do," The Man said. "You did name my dog for me, after all."

"Gatz," The Woman said admiringly of me with a happy little sigh.

"Gatz," The Man agreed, mirroring her emotions.

And . . . back to awkward silence.

Those silences were particularly difficult for me. If you don't keep me entertained every second we're in an eating establishment, it becomes that much harder for me to restrain myself from chasing down all the great food smells wafting through the air. And no matter how dog-friendly Nick's is, no one wants me hopping into strangers' laps to get closer to their freshly delivered, still-warm bread baskets.

"So," The Man said, taking an emergency gulp from his beer and only dribbling just a little bit, "I guess this is the part where a normal person would ask, 'SO! What do you do?'"

It's like a dual-edged sword. On the one hand, I appreciate that he's self-deprecating—nobody likes a guy who's unwarrantedly cocky—and that he knows himself. But on the other, does he have to out and out announce to people that he's not normal?

"I work in publishing," The Woman said, looking amused and like maybe she'd been harboring a secret. "I'm a book editor."

"Oh!" The Man said, sitting about as straight in his chair as he ever sits. "What a crazy coincidence. I'm a writer."

"I did know that."

"You knew that?"

"I recognized you right away."

"Recognized . . . me?"

"I've read all your books."

I could've knocked him over with my tail.

Before he could respond to this shocking bit of intel, The Woman leaned across the table and whispered, "You could say I'm a fan."

The Man was pleased, shocked, and embarrassed. You could say he was plockarrassed.

"Well, ah, ah—thank you! I, wow . . ." he said suavely.

"But don't worry," she added. "I'm not a dangerous fan, not a stalker or anything scary. It was pure luck running into you on the street like that."

He could see she was telling the truth: fan, yes; stalker, no— got it.

Uncomfortable and unused to having attention focused on him, let alone such beautiful attention, he parried back with a jovial,

"So, editing! Do you enjoy what you do?"

She gave the question careful consideration before a genuine smile broke across her face.

"You know," she said, "I really do. It's the perfect job for me. Except for those days when meetings seem endless, I love everything about it. I love finding great books, I love the work itself—the process of taking a manuscript and seeing it through until it's an actual book in bookstores. That moment you first see the book jacket you know is The One and all you can think is, 'Oh, so that's what you look like!'"

Anyone could see this was a woman who was passionate about her work. As for The Man, he was equally passionate about his work—the writing—but more quietly so.

"And oh!" she added. "The parties! I love going to industry parties. You never know who you're going to meet or what they're going to say. I only wish I'd been alive and doing this when Norman Mailer punched Gore Vidal in the face, to which Vidal, laid out on the floor, was rumored to have said something like, 'Words fail Norman Mailer yet again.' Are you familiar with that story?"

The Man was.

Although he did wonder: "So, you miss the days when the literary world was filled with brawls like the Saturday Night Fights?"

"No, not the violence. But I do love the colorfulness of it all. The passion about everything and the willingness to fight it all out, even if only metaphorically."

Dinner plates arrived, and when the waiter placed mine on the floor, I particularly appreciated that he crouched down to grate some last-minute strips of fresh Parmesan cheese over my warm meal. It's the extra little touches at Nick's that mean so much. As for the other two, there came the commencement of pasta being twirled on forks, The Man only getting a single spot of red sauce on his previously clean shirt.

"Wow," The Man said, "the parties. Yeah, no—the parties are the one thing I absolutely hate about being a published author. Being expected to show up at industry events, being expected to be 'on' all the time—you know? Not for me. If I could just write the books and never have to talk to another human being, I'd be the happiest man alive."

Then, perhaps realizing what a boneheaded thing he'd just said, he blushed.

"Present company excluded, of course!" he added hastily with a zeal that was just this side of manic.

Somehow, though, luckily, she was charmed.

For dessert, we all shared the cannoli.

Chapter Five

**Still a little less than three years ago,
but also just a tad closer to now . . .**

I had to wonder if the first time she saw his apartment, she experienced it the same way I'd experienced it the first time I'd seen it.

For me, it had been like, well, coming home.

After spending my early formative days in a small cage, I suppose anything would've felt like an improvement unless it was, you know, *less*. The Man's brownstone in Brooklyn, however, was beyond my wildest dreams. Space, but not too much space. The round table in front of the window with all the sunlight coming through it (great for barking at loud cars outside). The living area with the softest of chairs and comfy couch (that I would inevitably dig my teeth into when left alone too long). The kitchen stocked with enough items so that no one was ever going to starve, even if the kibble briefly ran out. The serviceable bathroom (site of future happy baths, after which an advanced case of the zoomies would always ensue) with the dampened toothbrush, proving that at least minimal laws of cleanliness would be adhered to. And the bedroom with its spacious bed, regarding which, immediately, he made me aware that my presence would always be welcome there.

It helped further that right after giving me the grand tour, we headed back out to the pet store, where he made sure I had food, treats, sturdy food and water bowls, toys, and a large cushioned pillow, just in case I wanted an alternative to the bed during daylight napping hours. Really, he made sure I had all the best doggy paraphernalia.

But no, I don't think The Woman's first experience of his apartment was the same.

After their initial evening at Nick's, they went on two more dates, both at Nick's. I didn't attend the third date. By that point, I just figured they needed some alone time, even if they weren't aware of needing it, and I feigned disinterest when it was time to go.

So, after that last one, about a week after the first, I was sleeping under the bed, curled up with one of The Man's flannel shirts—having shredded several of his other flannel shirts, because while I thought The Man and The Woman should have some alone time, I didn't necessarily want to *be* alone—when my ears perked up at the sound of the front door being unlocked. There was more than one lock. Hey, safety first.

Yawning and stretching, I was about to rouse myself to go greet him, knowing he'd want to perform the usual debriefing he had to go through after a date with The Woman by telling me every last word each of them said and how they looked at each other and what they ate—even though I'd been there to witness their first two dates for myself, thereby obviating any need for the old blow-by-blow account—when I heard a female voice whisper.

I realized then that for the first time since I'd been with him, The Man was not coming home alone.

What do I do? I wondered, finally understanding the feeling of awkwardness The Man perpetually experienced. *Do I go out there? Greet them both? I know what to do when it's just The Man—go right out—but what to do when it's two people? When The Woman's there too?* Oh, the dilemma. But something caused me to stay where I was, play things discreet.

I heard a series of sounds, not unlike when The Man would kiss my face after I licked him, but louder somehow, because human skin against human skin creates a sound louder than human skin against dog fur, which is much more subtle. If I had to describe the exact sound I was hearing, it would be *smooch*. A whole long series of smooches.

"Is this too soon?" I heard The Man say with characteristic caution.

"Not for me!" The Woman said with bold enthusiasm, followed by a slightly more cautious: "Why? Is it too soon for you?"

"NO!" The Man let out a near-yell that could only be described as overeager.

Another series of smooches followed, longer than the last, as I heard the sounds of feet—it sounded like sneakers and heels—making their stumbling way across the hardwood flooring in the living room and toward the bedroom. Fully alert now, instinct told me to stay in my spot, keeping as quiet as I could. I even went so far as to place my paws over my snout, so no one could hear me pant. If anyone was going to start panting tonight, it certainly wasn't going to be me.

At last, they were at the bedroom door. All I could see, from the soft glow of the living room light behind them, was their feet—I'd been right about the sneakers and high heels; but then, already I knew them both so well—and just a bit of their ankles as they approached the bed, their feet facing each other and so close together it was as though they were moving like one person.

I felt the mattress above me sag down closer to my face as they both sank down on the bed, and I saw their footwear leave their feet as though flying: There goes a sneaker, nearly hitting the door! There goes a high heel, sailing right out the doorway!

Then, with an "Oh!" The Man got up to shut the door separating the bedroom from the living area, and all there was, was sound.

But, oh, what sounds they were!

First came the sound of a zipper being pulled down, something I was familiar with from when The Man would remove his jeans. This zipper undoing, however, went much more excruciatingly slow—on his own, he was into a far more utilitarian and expedient fashion of garment removal—and from the amount of time taken, this seemed like it must be a far longer zipper, so I knew it couldn't be his. But then, soon after, I heard a short and quick zip, more like I was used to, and I figured: Hey! His pants are off!

More smooching, an acceleration of skin sounds, the occasional slurp—but not, you know, in a gross way—followed by the sound of something crinkly being torn open.

"Safety first?" I heard him whisper, a slight question at the end of his voice, like he was soliciting her input on it. Not the first time I'd ever heard him utter those words but definitely the most, well, solicitous.

"Safety first," she agreed with a soft, appreciative laugh, followed by more smooches.

Smooches, skin-on-skin sounds, grunts (but again, not gross), the occasional awkward laugh but somehow never embarrassed. It went on for a while, but somehow, at the same time, felt not long at all. In the end, there was a happy cry from her, almost immediately followed by a more forceful cry from him and . . .

Silence.

Just the sound of heavy breathing when it began to decelerate.

More silence.

Finally, from The Man, still sounding slightly out of breath but filled with wonder, "That was . . ."

And from The Woman, completely satisfied and affirmative, "That *was.*"

I couldn't say for certain what I'd just listened to, but whatever it was, it sure sounded like fun!

Plus, the smells were super interesting, even if I sensed that now was *not* the time for me to go around butt-sniffing, however great the temptation.

And somehow, I knew that I'd just borne witness to the beginning of something wonderful.

Chapter Six

Between less than three years ago and two and a half years ago . . .

Goin' courtin', goin' courtin'—kind of makes it sound like a musical from the '50s featuring a story that takes place in the 1800s, amiright? But that's exactly what it was like.

We took her out on *dates*. OK, maybe not *out* so much. But we had her over for takeout and movie nights. We took her for long walks, and on those long walks, we never expected her to scoop the poop. Even when she tried, we never let her. We even visited her one time in her place of business, because she invited us. And, here's a shocker. Even though everyone at the publishing company made a big fuss over me, they made an even *bigger* fuss over The Man. For the first time, I realized just what a well-respected big deal he was in literary circles and not just, you know, in his own mind.

And then there was the day we took her to *the* park. Not just any park, it was our favorite park. It was that day that I knew just how much she'd come to mean to him. You see, The Man loved to play fetch with me. Sometimes, I think he loved it even more than I did, if such a thing were possible. But on that day, I saw him hold himself back. I could visibly see him push down his own desire for his own pleasure as he offered her the stick.

And she took it.

Then she hurled the stick with all her might, and I chased after it with all my might, hearing her laugh delightedly behind me all the while. After I fetched and returned the stick to her, she offered it to The Man. But again, fighting his own no doubt overwhelming desire, he simply shook his head.

And so the day went on—she hurling, me fetching, all of us laughing—until we were all spent. For once in my life, for the *only* time in my life, a game of fetch had ended without me feeling afterward like: *It's over? How can it be over??? I THOUGHT IT WAS GOING TO GO ON FOREVER!!!*

But no, I was thoroughly satisfied, she was thoroughly satisfied, and even The Man, despite not playing fetch at all himself, was thoroughly satisfied too.

"That was the most fun I've had in," she gasped, laughing, then looking surprised as she added, "maybe ever."

We all collapsed on our backs on the grass then, and I listened, contentedly, as they talked for hours.

They talked about literature, they talked about life. They talked about how wonderful I was and how much they both loved me.

"And you," she said to The Man, surprising me by being the bold one to say it first. Not that she wasn't bold, but it takes a lot of chutzpah to jump from the high diving board without being sure if the person standing next to you is going to dive too. "I love you too."

"Is that the first time either of us has said it out loud?" The Man wondered.

She nodded, cautious for once.

"I'm sorry," The Man said. "I've been saying it in my head for so long, because I've been feeling it in my heart for so long, I was sure I'd said it out loud before, but I guess I haven't. I love you too."

She suggested that, to celebrate their vocalized love, they should go out to dinner.

"Nick's?" he said.

"Perhaps somewhere different?" she suggested. "Since it is a special occasion?"

Here's the thing about eating out. There were various breakfast spots The Man and I went to and cafés where we'd sit outside, contemplating the history of cappuccino and the mystery of life. There was even the trashy watering hole The Man favored for out-of-house beers. But as far as he was concerned, there was only one out-of-house place for dinner.

"There are other dog-friendly restaurants," The Woman pressed gently when he failed to respond right away.

"Of course," he said, visibly trying to be agreeable; open-minded, even. "And we've tried some of them. But here's the thing: even when they *say* they're dog-friendly, even when they *bill* themselves as being dog-friendly, none of them are as dog-friendly as Nick's."

You really couldn't fault his logic on this. Every word he spoke was true.

The Woman could see it too.

"Gatz does love their pasta," she said.

The Man nodded.

"And probably no one else in the city would crouch down to add extra fresh Parm to it for him," she added.

The Man shook his head.

"I love how much you love Gatz," The Woman said, "and I love him too." She took The Man's hand in hers. "Let's go to Nick's."

Chapter Seven

Two and a half years ago...

It was a hot August day, the kind of day where people flee the city rather than flocking to it.

But for me, never mind the blistering heat outside, it was the greatest day of my life thus far.

She's here! She's finally here! I would've shouted if only I could give voice to my thoughts as I ran around in circles. As it was, all I could do to show enthusiasm for this turn of events when I saw the U-Haul pull up outside our building was the running-around-in-circles part. I could only hope I was adequately conveying my delight at having her move in.

It's not like the idea of moving in the other direction, to her place in Manhattan, hadn't been entertained; seriously by her, more as a matter of fairness by him. To be honest, her place was nicer, bigger, and decorated with a more discerning eye. I knew, because I'd been there the few times she'd talked him into coming over and he'd brought me along. But let's face it: we all knew that a guy who could only rarely be persuaded to venture out for food rather than having it brought in wasn't the type of guy to take easily to uprooting all his own belongings, lock, stock, and doggy dish.

But that was OK! The moving van was here—it was finally here!—and we were all going to be together.

Seeing her jump out of the back of the van in sneakers, frayed blue jeans, tank top and with a babushka covering her hair, I must say, she'd never looked more beautiful.   •

It was all I could do to contain myself—OK, I couldn't contain myself, running around in circles like a maniac, chasing my own tail—as they pulled box after box out of the back of the van, hauling them up the stairs to the stoop and then inside.

You wouldn't think it would be easy to merge the contents of two households, but she was leaving nearly all her furniture behind. Rather than selling the condo, a gift from her parents, she was leasing it out completely furnished. So rather than a total rejiggering of everyone's stuff, it was more a matter of finding space for her coffee mug beside his coffee mug, her clothes beside his in the closet, and so forth. Once that was done, it was simply a matter of integrating their two book collections, a more difficult task than one might think—they were both very particular about how they arranged their book collections.

Finally, there was just one book left to find a place for, and luckily, there was a gap just its size. And so it was with a great sense of satisfaction that I watched—that he and I both watched—as she took her copy of *The Great Gatsby* and slid it in, shelving it right beside his decidedly more worn copy. When she adjusted it so the books were exactly aligned, it was perfect.

Then, the empty boxes stacked neatly near the front door, we three, we happy three—The Man, The Woman, and Gatz—collapsed in a joyful heap together on the couch.

One happy family, at last.

Chapter Eight

Two years and two months ago . . .

Is there any time of the year more fulfilling than the holidays?

The lights! The decorations! THE TREE! *THE WRAPPING PA-PER!!!*

The menorah.

Before the holidays that first year, The Man hadn't been in touch with his Jewish side very strongly. Honestly, I'd had no idea he even had a Jewish side.

But apparently, The Woman did. And she thought it was time he got in touch with it. Specifically, she thought it was high time he got in touch with his family.

Hanukkah came early that year, and with one thing on the schedule after another, it quickly became apparent that there would be no opportunity to go to The Man's family until the last night. This meant that we were on our own to open our presents for eight nights, which was fine by The Man and fine by me. I loved us together.

Turned out, The Man wasn't a great shopper. Oh, it's not like I don't think he tried. He did, for him. But he didn't like going out and didn't like shopping, which is not a great combination when it comes to gift giving. Even online shopping, it just wasn't for him. He might log onto Amazon with good intentions, but before you knew it, he'd lose patience. Before you knew it, he was looking at books instead. And before you knew it again, he was looking at his own books, specifically his Amazon rankings. Authors, man. They'll tell you they don't look at that stuff. But, trust me, they all do.

Anyway, here's the breakdown, as best I can recall, of what he got her for those eight nights: scarf, pen, scarf, chocolate, scarf, Starbucks gift card—not as impersonal as one might think, because she did love a good Iced Caramel Macchiato with extra drizzle—followed by the best present he gave her, a Yankees ball cap, that he'd purchased even though it killed him to do it because she'd once confessed that to the extent she followed baseball at all, she rooted for the Yankees, and that was opened with much glee all around on Night 7 and, finally, scarf.

And just to be clear, it's not like the scarves were thoughtless presents. If anything, like with so much else, he overthought it. "Gatz, blue is her favorite color, right? But which blue do you think she loves more, this blue or this blue?"

All I could do was bark my general approval. They all looked the same to me. So if, in the end, he got her nearly identical scarves, it wasn't like he didn't labor over it. It wasn't like he didn't care. He just didn't know how to be good at that kind of thing. As for the pen, what editor doesn't love a great pen? Honestly, if the ratio had been flipped—4:1 in favor of pens versus scarves, instead of the other way—it probably would've been better all around.

The Woman joked that people at work were going to start calling her Scarf Lady, but really, they were some bangin'-looking scarves. She wore them well and I knew she was happy. Plus, the Yankees ball cap really touched her, I could tell by the tears of joy in her eyes.

If he wasn't the best at shopping on his own, they were great shopping together. By this, I'm referring to what they jointly picked out for me. Each night, I ripped open the blue-and-silver wrapping to reveal a new toy: a ball; fake bones; lots of chewy rubber things to chew on—each more impressive than the last. It's not like I wasn't spoiled to begin with, but by the time those eight nights were over with, my toy basket runneth over.

And if he was just an OK shopper, if together they were great shoppers, on her own The Woman was the best shopper.

She knew what The Man loved best in the world, besides me and her, and gave it to him: books. Every night, a different book. These were super thoughtful books, ones she'd clearly taken a long time picking out.

And the way she presented them! The first night, she gave him a wrapped book-shaped object—no surprise there when it was opened. But the second night, she gave him a shirt-sized box, causing him to guess wrong before revealing another book. Night 3, an old-fashioned hatbox—oops, what's a book doing in there? By Night 4, even the dimmest bulbs amongst us had twigged to what was going on, and the biggest drama and most fun was in seeing what strange shape she'd conceal another great book within next. I thought Night 7—a giant refrigerator box, with so much wrapping paper to remove and the added benefit of a giant box for me to play in endlessly afterward until it fell apart—was really inspired.

The only glitch on her present-giving part came on Night 5, when he opened a triangular box to reveal . . .

"Commercial fiction?" he said, unable to hide his skepticism. "A bestseller? I don't usually read . . ."

"Don't be such a reading snob," she said, laughing. But when she said it, it didn't sound abrasive and insulting like it would if I said it. When she said it, it just sounded like good-natured advice. "He's a really talented writer."

"Of course," The Man said, smiling. "I trust your judgment. I'll give it a whirl."

Anyway, on Night 8, we were so sure it was going to be an eighth book, and we were totally OK with that, but we were puzzled as to what book would be so oblong and yet pancake flat.

Turned out not to be a book at all. Rather, she'd bought him a top-of-the-line laptop to replace the running-on-fumes laptop on the table by the window.

As much as he'd loved all the books, he was deeply touched by the thoughtfulness of this: she'd thought to do for him what he hadn't thought to do for himself.

They went to the bedroom to celebrate their joy over their gifts, making the sounds they always created when they were happy and making the smells they made when they were super happy, putting him in an even better mood, which turned out to be a good thing, because after that, it was time to go to his parents' place.

I'd naturally assumed we'd all be going together, but as they put on their winter coats while I panted eagerly by the door, The Man explained.

"I'm sorry, Gatz," he said, "but my mom just isn't a dog person. In fact, she's not a pet person at all, and my father's no better."

What kind of person doesn't like pets? I thought. *Not even a hamster? And how did you get to be so wonderful with me if you come from people who are bad with pets? And how come I've never even met your parents?*

"I'm sure it's not that bad," The Woman said.

"Trust me, it is." The Man turned to me. "Sure, you could come anyway. But I promise you, you'd just be made to feel uncomfortable, out of place. You're better off staying here, and we can tell you all about it when we get home."

I didn't like to be left on my own too much—I always wanted to go with if at all possible—but something in his suddenly grim expression kept me from insisting on going. So, I stayed. Whenever I got bored or lonely, I chewed on some sneakers, but not egregiously so.

I assumed they'd be gone for hours—we'd watched a lot of holiday movies together on the TV, and celebrations in them seemed to go on forever—but in a surprisingly short period of time, they were back.

"I told you," he said, throwing his coat down. It was the first time I'd ever heard him use such an admonitory tone with her. Plus, "I told you so" is never a good look for anyone, even when it's true.

"I know," she said, taking it well. It seemed like, rather than being offended and defensive, she just wanted to make it better for him. "And you were absolutely right. I shouldn't have insisted we go."

"What kind of a mother says to her author son: 'When are you going to write another real book?'"

As they talked more about it, I was able to suss this much out: The Man's mother had loved his first book, although he insisted he was pretty sure that was only because it gave her something to brag about; in fact, he was further sure she'd never read it, except maybe quickly to make sure none of the characters resembled her. But then with each new book he had published, she'd tell him it wasn't as good as the first, it wasn't *real*.

"What kind of person *does* that?" he said.

I could totally empathize, although for me, I was still stuck on: *What kind of person doesn't like pets?*

Then came a lot of "I know, baby" from The Woman, followed by a lot of "I'm sorry, I should've listened," and finally, "It'll be better when we go to my parents' for Christmas, I promise."

But *we* didn't go to her parents' for Christmas, emphasis on the *we*, not that year. By the time Christmas rolled around, it was apparent The Man was still so family-shocked—the relationship version of shell-shocked—from their brief sojourn with his over Hanukkah, he was all familied out for the year.

"The thing is," she said, "childish as it may sound, I've never been away from my family for Christmas. I'm just so close to them . . ."

She let the idea trail off.

But it wasn't allowed to trail off there for long, because almost immediately he rushed in to fill the silence with: "Of *course* you should still go see your family! Please don't stay here on my account. And, before you can say anything, I don't mean that in a passive-aggressive way at all."

I could tell he didn't, and I was sure she could tell too. It's impossible for The Man to fake anything. Sometimes, he might be better off if he could, but he just doesn't have it in him.

"I *want* you to go," he insisted, truthfully. "I would never want you *not* to have the holiday you deserve, just because of me and my hang-ups."

"If you're sure," she said.

"Absolutely," he said.

So, when the time came, she went, with promises to be back late Christmas Day night. But—surprise, happy surprise!—on Christmas Day morning, as we were eating our breakfast and reading the newspaper, we heard the key turn in the lock.

"Surprise, surprise!" she said.

"What are you doing back early?" The Man asked. "Was it"— he paused, as though remembering times with his own family— "bad?"

"Of course not!" she said. "It was *wonderful*. I got to see everyone and spend time with them all, but then this morning, after we opened our presents, I realized I was missing you both too much, so I came home early. I hope that's OK."

OK? It was more than OK!

We three were all in agreement about just how OK it was as we rolled around on the floor together, laughing.

So maybe The Man hadn't gone to The Woman's family with her. The Woman was OK with this.

I was OK with this. We'd had our eight nights of wonderful presents earlier in the month and our beautiful menorah that The Woman had bought with its colorful fast-dripping candles and bright flames. And now we had our tree that could've come out of an advertisement and that we'd decorated with great love and good humor, even when it took a while to get the lights to light—honestly, I thought our tree could rival the one they showed on TV at Rockefeller Center, even if ours was a little smaller.

Menorah; tree.
The Man; The Woman.
Me.
All of it a perfect fit.
All was right in the world.

Chapter Nine

One year and two months ago...

The holiday season had rolled around again, still a joyous time, what with the scarves, the books, the toys. The tree was looking good, and the menorah remained untarnished.

But after the fiasco with The Man's family the year before, it was decided they'd just go to The Woman's family this time. I curled up on my fluffy doggy bed, accepting of the need to sometimes be left behind, but then The Woman called to me from the doorway.

"Come on, Gatz. Time to go."

"But won't they mind?" The Man objected.

"Of course not," she said. "Who could mind Gatz?"

Right? That's what I say: Who could mind Gatz?

And her parents, in their fancy high-rise apartment, didn't mind me, not even when we exited the penthouse elevator straight onto the plush white carpeting.

"Shouldn't we do something about his feet first?" The Man said, worried.

But as he bent to wipe off my paws with the handkerchief he kept handy for those times we entered stores that didn't look immediately ecstatic to see us, a stunning woman of a certain age with a martini glass containing a beverage that matched the color of her impeccable magenta suit hurried over on stocking feet, waving him away.

"Don't worry about that," she dismissed, followed by: "Gatz! Oh, I've so longed to meet you. I'm just glad you're finally here!"

Let me tell you, I was the hit of the party.

The Woman's parents; her two brothers, their wives and kids; other assorted guests—no one could get enough of good old Gatz. Even when, in my enthusiasm at being the center of such a large group of attention, my tail accidentally knocked a Baccarat crystal bowl of cocktail sauce all over the pristine white carpeting, no one seemed to mind.

"Don't be silly," The Woman's mom said as The Man frantically tried to sop it up. "If the house cleaner can't get the stain out, we'll just get a new carpet. Really, it's no problem."

I could tell it wasn't, for her. But The Man? I could tell he was still bothered by it and, well, everything else.

Everyone tried to make him feel welcome; they certainly made me feel welcome. They asked him questions about his work. And these weren't the kind of stupid questions writers get asked all the time, the ones I knew The Man hated, like "Where do your ideas come from?" and "What are you working on next?" when you'd just finished a book; I mean, come on, give a guy a break—we're not making widgets here. Nor were these just pro forma, we're-being-polite-but-we-really-don't-know-what-we're-talking-about-nor-do-we-really-care questions. Well, of course these people asked great writing-related questions—they all knew and loved The Woman, and The Woman was an editor, for crying out loud!

And oh, how they did love The Woman.

It was apparent in everything they said and did. And almost instantly, I felt like they loved me too.

I was sure they'd love The Man as well, if only he'd let them; if only he'd meet them, never mind halfway, even if he met them a hundredth of the way, they'd be all in.

But he just couldn't do it.

Oh, he was polite enough, answering every question—but they were minimal answers, with minimal enthusiasm, everything minimal.

If I could have, I would've screamed at him: *Try! Why can't you at least try?*

But he just couldn't. Certainly, he wouldn't, didn't.

In the end, we were the first to leave the party, The Woman making our excuses as we went, blaming it on herself: "So much going on at work . . . this monster book to edit . . . wish we could stay . . ."

When we got home, it was apparent the evening had taken a lot out of The Man.

"That took a lot out of you, didn't it?" The Woman said, always a sharp observer.

"It did," he allowed, grabbing himself a beer. "I told you, I'm not good at social things."

OK, buddy, I thought, *this is the part where you add, "But I'm so sorry and I'll try to do better. If it's important to you, it's important to me. I'll really try to do better."*

But he didn't.

She acted like she didn't mind that we'd left early. I acted like I didn't mind that we'd left early.

The menorah, the tree.

Him, her, and me.

It was still a pretty good Christmas.

Chapter Ten

Two months ago . . .

I'd be lying if I didn't say the glow had gone out of the holidays, *just a little bit.*

Oh, we still had the menorah, still had the tree. But this year, instead of multicolored candles for the menorah, they were just one color—blue—and instead of standing straight in the menorah, they tended to list to the side, listing so hard that a lit one even toppled over once. It probably would've burned the whole place down if I hadn't been vigilant; if I hadn't barked with all my doggy might as soon as I saw what was happening, barking loudly until they finally came running.

As they doused the small flames with water, I thought: *You should've been watching. You both should've been paying better attention* and *Couldn't you have just doused the flames on the table but somehow kept the candles lit? Couldn't you have saved it? I'm pretty sure you're supposed to let the candle flames go out naturally.*

If the Hanukkah candles were all askew, the Christmas tree fared no better. Some of the ornaments couldn't be found, and this year, when the lights wouldn't immediately light, no one took the time to stay on the job until success was achieved. They just didn't bother.

Half-assed candles; half-assed tree. The Man and The Woman feigned enthusiasm, but I could tell neither was invested in the process anymore.

It didn't help that he'd bought her eight scarves this year, which, as they say, is a scarf too far—even I could see that—and two of the scarves were the same, just in a different shade.

But that was OK! Things still could've been OK, because if they were at least feigning, it meant they were still trying, on some level. *It will all work out in the end*, I thought, until . . .

The Man was sacked out on the couch; The Woman out of sight in the kitchen, just a disembodied voice. Me, I was keeping a wary eye on things from the bedroom doorway.

"Two years ago," The Man said, "you insisted we go to my family."

"I don't know if 'insisted' is the word I'd use . . ."

"Fine. You're the editor."

"That's right. I am the editor."

"Fine," he said again. "Last year, you persuaded me to go to your family."

"'Persuaded' doesn't strike me as accurate either."

"Whatever."

Wait. Did he just *whatever* her? Oh, this was bad, very bad. Sometimes, it's impossible for two people in a relationship to come back from an ill-timed *whatever*. It's a well-documented fact.

Sure enough, deadly silence from the kitchen, only broken when The Man said:

"How about this year, we go to *no* families? Would no families work for everybody?"

Oh crap, buddy. I put my paws over my head in disgrace. *It would've been better if you'd just let the silence go. It would've been better if you hadn't broken it. Don't you know by now that it's better to keep silent and have everyone think you're a fool than open your mouth and confirm it? I mean, I love you, man, but come on: Surely, even you can see that this is not the route to go right now, can't you? So let's all take some deep, calming breaths and—*

BANG! A kitchen cabinet slammed, the cabinet obviously not do-

ing the slamming on its own. And with that startling slam, I lifted my
head from my paws, on high alert now.

"Spending time with family during the holidays," The Woman
said, causing me to swivel my head toward the kitchen, "*it's what
people do.*"

The way she bit off those last four words; the steel in her voice—oh,
this was all bad, very bad.

"Well," The Man said, indicating himself with a hard thumb jab
that seemed pointless since The Woman wasn't there to witness it,
just me; I mean, why make the effort?—"not thi**s** people!"

Even though she was far away in the kitchen, I could hear her
sigh—perhaps she no longer found his awkwardness charming; and I
sadly confess that, in the moment, I wasn't finding him as charming
as usual either—but if he heard the sigh too, he gave no sign as he
continued.

"And while we're on the subject . . ."

Not "*while we're on the subject,*" I groaned inwardly. I'd seen people
"while we're on the subject" other people on TV before. It never ends
well. It only adds fuel to the fire.

Sure enough, the implied threat of "while we're on the subject"
was enough to draw from the kitchen The Woman, looking angrier
than I'd ever seen her, as The Man swung his legs down, rising from
the couch.

"And while we're on the subject," he repeated, now that she was
in the room with him, "do we really have to go to your company's
holiday party or your friend's New Year's Eve party this year? Do we
have to go to any parties together, ever again?"

"No," she said, still angry. "We don't."

"Good," he said, visibly relieved.

"We don't ever have to go to parties, or anywhere else together,
ever again."

"Wait. What?"

I was right there with him. Wait. What? Let's not get carried away here . . .

Her angry energy swiftly turned to sadness as she spoke again.

"I didn't know it was going to be like this."

"Like what?" he said. "I told you what I was like from the beginning."

"You did," she admitted, still sad.

"But you thought, what, that you might change me?"

"No, not that, never that. I guess I simply thought that you'd eventually want to change. For me . . . for us. That you'd be happy to compromise and happy going out, going to parties—at least sometimes—because it meant being with me."

"I love being with you. I'm happy being with you."

She smiled at that, if only just a little smile, perhaps thinking that he was going to go somewhere else with this.

But he didn't.

"The thing is, though, I don't *need* anyone else. Just you. And Gatz."

And back to sadness, a deeper sadness as she said, "That's the problem. I love you, but I need other people too."

"And what does *that* mean?" The Man demanded, still in angry mode, still not getting it, still not seeing how precariously we were teetering on the edge here.

Come on, guys! I wanted to bark at them both, vehemently. *Let's just take this thing down a notch—two notches even! We'll all just calm down, have a seat, and—*

"I think it means," The Woman said slowly, "we're over."

As though he'd been slapped, The Man looked instantly shocked, devastated.

We were over? How could we be over?

Chapter Eleven

Later that same day . . .

It's amazing how quickly disaster can strike. One minute you're there living your life, happily drinking champagne from your doggy bowl, chasing your tail under the stars, the world your leftover piece of turkey, beautiful horizon as far as the eye can see. The next thing you know, there's an iceberg right in front of you and—bam!—your un-sinkable ship is going down, all is lost.

I know because I saw it on *Titanic*.

After all their time together, it was amazing how little time it took her to amass her things and put them in a few boxes: her mug, her bathroom stuff, some of her clothes.

"I'll get the rest of my clothes later, if that's OK," she said.

"Fine," he said, tight-lipped.

How many relationships, in the history of the Universe, have been further sunk by a tight-lipped "fine"?

"Where will you go?" he said.

"To my folks'," she said. "It'll only be for a few days anyway. As luck would have it, the sublease on my apartment is out soon. Then I'll move back there."

"It runs out in a few days? Were you planning this?"

"No," she said, stung. "God, no."

He relented, seeing the harm he'd caused. "You could stay here," he offered, "for those few days, wait until—"

"No," she said softly.

"No," he agreed, "I guess you're right. When it's over . . ."

". . . it's over," she finished for him, sounding hopelessly, devastatingly sad.

I'll tell you when I knew it was over. When I looked over at the bookshelves and noticed the gap between books: her copy of *The Great Gatsby* was no longer there, no longer lined up perfectly right next to his. When I'd gone for a quick sip from my water bowl—all the fighting had made me anxious, and anxiety makes me thirsty, and then drinking too much makes me have to pee—she must've removed it. It must now be there in one of those boxes. The boxes that were leaving us. With her.

She gave one final glance around the room, perhaps taking note of her own future absence, before turning and reaching for the door.

"*WAIT!*" The Man shouted as the door swung open, causing her to turn back.

Yes! I thought. *YES!* This was the part where he'd fall to his knees, profess his undying love, pledge to do better, *be* better. He'd remind her of that one time they went to a Subway Series game together, sitting side-by-side in their respective Mets and Yankees caps, and how romantic it was when the Kiss-Cam zeroed in on them in full lip-lock—I know because I watched it all from home on the TV.

And it wouldn't all be one-sided, because then she'd fall to her knees too. She'd take his hands in hers and apologize for her role in their mutual problems, and she'd also promise to do better, be better, and then they'd kiss a lot and go do that thing in the bedroom that makes the mattress rock, and we'd all be happy together forever and ever, and—

"You love him too," The Man said.

"What?" she said.

"Gatz. It's not fair for me to get to keep Gatz entirely. You love him too."

That's right, I barked triumphantly. *It's not fair for any one person to get to keep Gatz entirely. So you two have to stay together!*

"But you loved him first," The Woman said. "It would be even less fair for me to take him from you."

First, schmirst—just stay together and it won't matter who loved who first!

"Still," The Man said. "You were there from the very first day. How about if I kept him Mondays through Fridays because you're at work all day and sometimes don't get home until late . . ."

"And I could take him on weekends?" she said, with a grateful relief.

He nodded.

"And holidays too?" she asked, hopeful now.

The Man paused, eventually nodding. "Holidays too."

"Joint custody?" The Woman said.

"Joint custody," The Man agreed.

They even broke up with love! See? They were *meant* for each other!

Chapter Twelve

Six and a half weeks earlier...

Is there any time of the year sadder than the holidays?

The menorah was still out. Without her there to remind him, he hadn't bothered to put it away.

The tree was still up too, although the only presents under it this year had been for me, and those had long since been opened, admired, and put away in my toy basket.

I'd spent Christmas with her per their joint-custody agreement. We spent both Eve and Day with her family. I can't say it was a bad time. Everyone made a fuss over me, and I appreciated their fussing. Nor did they object when, left to my own devices for a smidge too long, I shredded all the Kleenex in the fancy guest bathroom. They even put some roast beef on a fancy plate next to my water bowl. Who could object to that? But I'd missed The Man. Worse, I'd worried about him. What was he doing back in the apartment all alone? I knew he wouldn't go anywhere, nor would he have anyone in. I had all these happy people around me, while he'd just be alone.

When The Woman dropped me off, he greeted me like I usually greeted him whenever he walked through the door, no matter how briefly he'd been out: like he'd been gone forever. Then he told me everything he'd done while I'd been gone. It didn't take long.

"I wrote, Gatz!" he said. Then he waved a sheaf of freshly printed pages in my direction. "Do you have any idea how much writing a person can get in when there are no interruptions?"

Yeah, I did know. He'd just waved that big sheaf of pages at me, hadn't he?

But who knew if whatever he'd written was any good or if it all just sucked? I certainly didn't look closely at the pages. For all I knew, he'd simply spent twenty-four hours typing "All work and no play makes The Man a very dull boy" over and over again.

Perhaps worried he might have caused offense, he hastened to add, "Of course, I didn't mean you, boy. You're never an interruption. Hey, I hope you had a good time. I really hope they took good care of you over there."

Then he gave me a healthy scratch under the chin for good measure.

Well, he certainly sounded like he'd managed fine enough on his own. Still, when I saw the single bowl and spoon in the draining rack, and the empty cereal box on the counter—it'd been full when I left—and the quantity of empty beer bottles in the recycle bin, I realized he'd subsisted on cereal and beer in my absence. Then I felt guilty. I knew it wasn't my fault, but there I'd been living high on the hog with roast beef while he was knocking back the cereal and brewskis? And that lone bowl and spoon, where once there'd been two—somehow, it just struck me as pathetic.

Next would be New Year's—another chance for pathetic.

So imagine my surprise when The Man informed me that The Woman informed him that she thought it would be better for him to have me for New Year's, or at least fairer. She told him that while she knew they'd agreed I would be with her on the holidays, with Christmas and New Year's being holidays that fell just a week apart, it didn't seem fair that she should have me for both.

"What do you think?" The Man asked me. "Will that be OK with you, Gatz?"

I'm ashamed to admit that I did think longingly of that roast beef. But the longing passed quickly. Mostly, I was just relieved he wouldn't be on his own. Because while she had all those other people, he only had me.

Then New Year's Eve hit, and as the day of the eve drew on, I felt a . . . *mood* take me. At first, I couldn't pinpoint it, but as I listened to The Man pound away on his keyboard, writing excitedly at the table while I sacked out on the floor beside him, I recognized what that mood was: for the first time in my life, I was depressed.

"Isn't this great, Gatz?" he enthused.

Pound, pound, pound.

Sure. Great.

"Just the two of us?"

Pound, pound, pound.

Whoop-de-do. Color me unimpressed.

"Yup, just the two of us!" Was it just me or did this guy sound a touch manic? And who was he trying to convince—me or himself? "This is . . . great."

A couple of hours later, there I was in the same position—slumped into the carpet, limbs outstretched, tongue tucked inside mouth, tail still, ears droopy—having barely moved in the time that had passed. The only difference was that now I had a party hat slapped on my head—The Man's doing; remnants of the few things The Woman had left behind. I guessed she'd have new party hats wherever she was tonight.

The Man was still working the "Just the two of us—isn't this great?" angle as he clicked on the TV to watch the countdown as the ball dropped at Times Square. Without her there to guide him, The Man had turned on Ryan Seacrest. Didn't he know by now that The Woman and I preferred Anderson Cooper and Andy Cohen? Not to mention, watching Don Lemon get progressively drunker is always a hoot. But apparently, The Man hadn't been paying attention to details like that over the years. I guess there are some guys who just don't.

As cheers came pouring from the TV—with thousands and thousands of revelers screaming, "Three! Two! One! Happy New Year!"—The Man looked over at me. We were mirror images of depression: him, sunk into the couch; me, sunk into the carpet.

"You're right, Gatz," he conceded. "This sucks."

Indeed.

Chapter Thirteen

Yesterday...

And just for the record: No. Yesterday my troubles did not feel so far away.

I was lying on the couch, chewing on my own tail, when The Man walked in the front door.

"Hey, buddy," he said. "Sorry I took so long."

He had a bag with him, and after petting me on the head, which I happily let him do, he removed a red heart-shaped box from the bag, setting it down on the round writing table by the window. I'd seen boxes like that before. He always bought them for The Woman. He may not have been big on most holidays, but he did have his romantic side.

For a brief moment, my heart leaped in my chest. Maybe they were getting back together already?

But then, as The Man puttered around the apartment, my attention zeroed in more closely on that box. Somehow the boxes he had got for her were always more impressive: bigger, prettier, just all-around nicer. While this one, this was just . . . *utilitarian*.

If he thought he was going to woo her back with this . . .

"Yeah, I know," The Man said, "it's a little early."

A little early for *what*?

This wasn't too early, not at all. As far as I was concerned, he should've been trying to get back together with The Woman the day after she left.

"I don't even know if I like her!" The Man continued.

Well, of course he liked her—she was The Woman!

"I know I just started seeing her—"

Wait. What?

"But if you're dating someone when Valentine's Day rolls around, even if it's only been a little while, you kind of have to get them a box of chocolates. I mean, unless the person is allergic or just told you they're on a diet, in either of which cases, it would be cruel. But outside those exceptions, isn't that what people do?"

He was looking to me for dating advice?

And wait. We were seeing people? We were seeing other people? When did *that* happen?

And then it hit me. Not long after the most depressing New Year's Eve ever, he'd brought some woman home one night. I guess despite his always saying he preferred to be alone, he didn't mean *that* alone. Some people doth protest too much. But I hadn't felt before like she was a serious threat to The Man and The Woman getting back together, even after she came home with him a couple of other times. As far as I could tell, all they ever did was shake the mattress together a bit. They hardly talked; there was no happy laughter; even the smells were off. She never even stayed for breakfast. It all struck me as somehow . . . *transactional*. Still . . .

"I mean," The Man said, "I wouldn't even call what we do 'dating' necessarily. I just figured . . ."

His words trailed off as he shook his head, heading off toward the bedroom, and I knew the depression had overtaken him again, the depression he'd been experiencing on and off since The Woman left.

I eyed that menacing heart-shaped box, my brain going double-time.

Even if The Man was dismissive about the intended recipient of the heart-shaped box, this was getting too close for comfort. It didn't sound like this woman he was dating, but not dating, meant anything to him. And I doubted he meant anything to her either. But it was still too close for comfort. The Man and The Woman were no nearer to reuniting than they had been two months ago.

These were drastic times. They called for drastic measures.

I needed to do something about this!

Chapter Fourteen

And back to Valentine's Day...

There I was, still feeling like I was at death's door, as The Man and The Woman faced off over my supine body.

"Valentine's Day chocolates?" The Woman said, stung. "Who are those for?"

"Nobody," The Man said, shooting the word out of his mouth just about as quickly as it was possible to shoot a word.

If my physical condition weren't so dire, I would've barked vociferously to underscore his "nobody." I would've tried to indicate just how nobody this other woman was: *They don't talk! They don't laugh! She doesn't stay for breakfast! It's just some mattress shaking!* But as it was, all I could manage was a pathetic whimper.

"Nobody?" she echoed. "Seriously? I'll bet she doesn't think so." She paused. "Maybe it's time I started seeing 'nobody' too."

Despite my weakened state, my eyes went wide at this.

Nope. This was not what I'd been hoping to achieve.

Not. At. All.

Chapter Fifteen

Five weeks later ...

There are some things I know, because when women talk, I always listen. I *always* pay attention.

We were in The Woman's high-rise apartment, which is exactly as orderly as everything else in her life, but not without its touches of personality; I particularly appreciate her colorful collection of soft throw pillows, which, out of respect, I never throw.

It was the weekend, I'd long since fully recovered from my Valentine's Day ordeal, The Woman had picked me up the day before, and now we were hosting that wine-soaked monthly event otherwise known as Book Club.

Assembled were me, The Woman, and three of her coworker friends: The Redhead, The Blonde, and The Brunette. Since it was the weekend, everyone was super cazh, with not a pencil skirt or blazer in sight. The four women were all arranged on the couches and chairs, industrial-sized goblets of wine in hand. Me, I was respectfully lounging on the carpeting near their feet, waiting for the stimulating intellectual conversation to begin. And maybe I was waiting for some of the nacho dip to fall. When they get enough wine in them, there are always drips.

You'd think that, working on and talking about and living and breathing books all week long, they'd want to do something—anything—else with their time. Like, I'm pretty sure cabdrivers don't spend their days off gleefully going for joyrides. But such was not the case here. These ladies couldn't get enough of books. Or wine.

"So," said The Blonde, an editor on equal footing with The Woman at their publishing company but without, I'd been told by The Man, her discerning eye, "who read the book?"

Here's where I need to point out that, traditionally speaking, not a whole lot of talking-about-the-specific-book goes on at Book Club. I know, a cliché, but still. This particular group does talk about books a lot—but those are ones they're editing and publishing. They also talk about families, romantic relationships, food, parties, movies, and TV, not necessarily in that order. Still, for show, even though no one but me can see them, they usually attempt more than one specific-book-related question before diving into other subjects. But on that night . . .

"I think I might've . . . met someone last weekend," The Woman said. "A new man."

At this, my ears perked up.

New Man? *Met* someone last weekend? What did we do last weekend? Oh right. I hadn't been with her. I'd stayed behind with The Man, while she went off to that stupid book fair . . .

Picture a grand building, packed with business professionals.

Picture a stage, upon which is a long table, behind which is a super large sign reading LONDON BOOK FAIR and below that, in only slightly smaller lettering, AUTHOR/EDITOR PANEL.

A large audience is there for the panel, which is composed of four author/editor pairings plus a moderator. The center two author/editor pairings are comprised of The Woman and her author—Hispanic female, flannel shirt open over a tank top and jeans, baseball cap on backward—and someone we might as well start calling New Man and his editor. Really, no one in the room but these four people matters very much. Come to think of it, only two of them do. It is further worth noting that New Man is in his early thirties, suave, Asian, debonair, beautiful—honestly, if he's not actually Henry Golding, he might as well be. The only thing marring his features is the faintest of scars beneath one eye, but even that can't be called a flaw, because, like the slight gap in The Woman's own front teeth, that one tiny imperfection only serves to add to the overall impression of beautiful perfection.

And . . . scene.

"OK, last question," the moderator said. "This one is for the editors: What do you see as being your single most important responsibility within the author/editor relationship?"

Immediately, The Woman leaned into her mic, and when she spoke, it was just to say one word: "Invisibility."

"I'm a bit puzzled," the moderator said, "and I suspect the audience is too. Could you elaborate on that a bit, please?"

"Of course," The Woman said. "My job is to help my authors make whatever book is in question the best it can possibly be. To do that, I need to clearly identify where I think changes should be made and, further, prescriptions for how those improving changes might be achieved. Then it's up to the author—because, in the end, the book is always the author's book; not the editor's, not the publisher's—to decide which ideas to adopt and which to reject. And all of this must be done seamlessly so that once the book is published, no one should be able to tell, nor should the author even remember, where one of us left off and the other began. Like I said: invisible."

The moderator nodded his approval as the audience clapped politely, perhaps not quite getting it. One person who did seem to be getting it, fully, was New Man, who'd leaned forward as her short speech progressed, gazing at her with admiration and appreciation as though to say: *Where have you been all my life?*

"Anyone else on the panel care to comment?" the moderator prompted.

"Yes," said New Man's editor, who had too much gel in his slicked-back hair and was wearing a skinny suit that was just the slightest bit of shine shy of being sharkskin. He hooked a manicured thumb at New Man as he said, "Well, my most important job is making sure *this guy* gets to places like this on time."

New Man's editor laughed at his own joke, and the audience laughed with him, clapping as The Woman and New Man exchanged tight smiles.

"I think getting *this guy* here on time is an endeavor we're all appreciative of," the moderator said. "After all, he is one of our most popular bestselling authors!" The audience roared their approval. "Thanks for coming, everybody! 'Dystopian Among Us' starts in twenty minutes!"

Everyone on the panel rose from their seats, heading off the stage.

The Woman turned to her author, who immediately hugged her, The Woman hugging her right back.

"I just love working with you," the author said.

"It's mutual," The Woman said.

"How did I ever get so lucky?"

"Please. The pleasure is all mine."

"Will I see you at the party later on tonight? Please tell me you're coming. I need you there. You know how I hate those things."

"I promise. Don't worry, I'll be there. I wouldn't miss it for the world."

As the author moved off, The Woman sensed a presence behind her. Turning, she was startled to find New Man standing there, but not in an unpleasant way, not like a candidate lurking behind a rival in the hopes of intimidating that rival during a debate. Rather than speaking to his own crowd of waiting admirers, he'd clearly been waiting eagerly and patiently to speak to her. Tall as she was in her heels, standing up, he was even several inches taller. Despite his suave demeanor, he almost looked nervous, which became apparent when he spoke.

"Hey," he said, "that was, um, that was really amazing what you said up there."

"Oh, well, thank you," The Woman said, feeling unaccountably flustered. She was used to feeling confident in her work and that whatever praise she garnered for it was well-earned. "I think that—"

But before she could finish stating just what exactly she did think, New Man's editor—who'd himself turned away from his author upon completion of the panel to see what other big fish there might be to fry—pounced, as though his radar had immediately shot all the way up.

"Hey," he said with a smile that was more a warning than a welcome, "you're not trying to poach my author, are you?"

The Woman was stunned silent by this accusation, while New Man looked at his editor with cool exasperation.

"Nobody is trying to poach anybody," he said. "Why don't you hit the food table and I'll join you in a moment."

"All right, buddy, but don't take too long," New Man's editor said; and to The Woman: "Always a pleasure!"

The Woman nodded along as though she shared that sentiment, but you could tell she wasn't really feeling it.

Once his editor was out of earshot, New Man turned his interest back on The Woman.

"You started to say, 'I think that,'" he said. "I'd really like to hear more. In fact, I'd like to hear more about everything that you think." He made a facepalm motion. "Oh, god. That was too much, wasn't it? Like, totally smarmy, right?"

The Woman nodded, but inside, she was charmed. It was endearing that someone whose public persona was embodied by a James Bond–like suaveness could become flustered by her.

"Let me try again," New Man started. "Is there any chance you'd let me buy you dinner tonight?"

Here, she hesitated. "Your editor already accused me—unwarrantedly,

I might add—of trying to poach you. I fear if you had dinner with me instead of him, it might tip his paranoia right over the edge."

"And I'd invite him to join us, but I happen to know he's already made other plans. He's a bit like that, always keeping his eye out for something better. Honestly, you'd be doing me a huge favor, since I hate dining alone."

"Oh, I'm sure there is no shortage of booksellers and librarians who would love to have dinner with you."

"Perhaps, but I liked what you said on the panel and was hoping to get your professional advice . . ."

The restaurant he took her to that evening was not at all like Nick's, which, over the course of three years, was pretty much the only restaurant The Man had ever taken her to. This restaurant was upscale—a see-and-be-seen sort of place—and yet it was clear from the maître d's comments that New Man had called ahead, arranging for an intimate table where they could see but not be seen. As they walked to that intimate table, it was further clear that both had taken care with their appearance, everything a step above the business attire common to book fairs; a strong effort had been made. Well, she did have that party to get to later. He probably had his own party to get to as well.

At the table, New Man confidently pulled out her chair for her and, graciously, she let him.

Drinks ordered, New Man opened the conversation with, "You know, I really did love what you said today, about what you see as the editor's role."

"And I meant every word of it," The Woman said.

"I could tell that you did," New Man said appreciatively. "It strikes me that some might think it odd that I should be so enchanted by your stated desire to be invisible. But, of course, you strictly meant that editorially—I know we just met but already I can't imagine you being invisible in any other way—and it further strikes me that one must have a wonderfully healthy level of self-confidence to have the attitude you do."

The Woman smiled at the compliment, her self-confidence on vivid display, but said nothing.

"Oh gosh," he groaned. "I'm doing it again, aren't I? Trying too hard? Coming on too strong?"

The Woman smiled, holding her index finger and thumb so close, there was barely any space between them.

He groaned again. "That's what I thought."

"Maybe you'd get in less trouble if you stuck to business, leaving the personal compliments out of it. This was supposed to be strictly a business dinner, wasn't it?"

"Right you are: business." He cleared his throat.

"In my experience," New Man continued, "editors usually want to put their own fingerprints on everything, trying to achieve the exact opposite of what you said your goal is—editorial invisibility—so that afterward, they can tell people that the author would be nowhere without them." He paused. "I do know that's a sweeping generalization and that not all editors are like that, that most are good people doing their jobs earnestly, most falling somewhere along the vast continuum between the Svengalis at one end of the spectrum and all the way at the other end, you. But there are enough Svengalis to leave me with the occasional bad taste."

They paused as the waiter came to take their food orders.

After the waiter departed, New Man continued with a rueful look at his wine, "And then there's my editor . . ."

"Yes," The Woman said, knowingly and yet noncommittally, "I've met him."

"You know," New Man said, "I've loved everything about my publishing experience." He took a sip of his wine before setting the glass down and toying with the stem between his fingers. "Except for that."

"What are you saying?" The Woman asked, still noncommittal.

"What if I told you," New Man said, "that I want to be poached?"

The Woman was on full alert now, but said nothing, waiting.

"What if I told you I wanted to be poached by you?"

The Woman started to smile. One of the most successful novelists in the world wanted to work with her? What editor wouldn't be flattered by that? But then the smile froze.

"That's exactly what your editor accused me of. We can't be having this discussion."

"Then how about if I tell you a story about another author. Would that be OK?"

"Not if it's of the 'I have a friend who' variety when everyone knows the 'friend' is the person speaking."

"It's not like that at all. Do you know who Robert Ludlum is? Or was? Since he's dead and yet books keep coming out with his name on them."

She rolled her eyes, but not unkindly. She worked in publishing, she loved books, of course she knew who Robert Ludlum was: one of the greatest spy novelists of the previous century.

"Right," he said, looking embarrassed. "Of course you do. Anyway, an old bookseller once told me a story about him. Apparently, he was a customer of hers. And she said that despite all the riches his best-sellers had provided him with, it was her opinion that the one book that made him happiest was the more humorous one he'd written earlier in his career. That it was her further belief that he'd have been happier if he could have done more of that."

"So, what are you saying? That you want to write spy novels? Or humorous fiction? But you do neither."

"No, that's not what I'm saying at all. I'm saying I'm tired of doing the same stupid pet trick over and over again, no matter how lucrative. I'm saying I want to do a different stupid pet trick." He leaned forward here. "Look, I don't want to do anything drastically different. I don't want to completely reinvent my own wheel. And I'm not complaining about the lifestyle that being successful has blessed me with. But I am saying that I do want to write books with more depth to them."

The penny finally dropped. "And your editor isn't supportive of that."

New Man pointed his trigger finger at her. "Got it in one. Not only is he not supportive, he doesn't want it at all! He says it would, and I quote, 'spoil the brand.'"

"But you're not talking about wanting an entire genre change, are you?"

He shook his head.

"You just want to write with more depth. Who could object to that?"

New Man shrugged. "Tell that to my editor." He paused. "Or better yet, *be* my editor." He paused again. "You know, I've read several of the books you've edited. It's such a wonderful range of books you've worked on. I'm a huge fan."

The Woman hadn't sought this out. She would never have sought this out. But it had come to her. And what could be more attractive to an editor than a stupendously successful author wanting to write even better books and believing that she was the best editor to help him do so?

"But what about your contract?" she said.

"That's the beauty of it: I've delivered all the books I owe them," New Man said. "The latest book I attempted, the one I really wanted to write, was my option book. And since my editor already said no to that, that they'd prefer I write something else 'more on brand' . . . "

"I'm not entirely comfortable talking about this any further right now. Perhaps, if you really are serious about this—"

He nodded, vigorously, almost like a puppy.

"If you are truly serious," she said more forcefully, "then have your agent get in touch with me. And we'll see what happens from there."

And that was that.

Over their food, they talked about other-than-publishing things: families, hobbies, life.

At one point, he not-so-subtly asked her if she lived alone.

"Yes," she said.

"I do too," he said.

"Well," she added, "except for Gatz, but that's only on weekends."

A handsome eyebrow was raised. "Gatz? Is that your . . . son?" He didn't say it like it was a problem, more like just a matter of curiosity.

"Of sorts." She laughed. "Gatz is my dog, a border collie. I share custody of him with my ex."

"And how does that work?"

"Better than you might think. Do you like dogs?"

"Of course," he said, his finger going to the tiny scar beneath his eye, the finger-to-scar move an occasional tic. "Who doesn't love dogs?"

An hour later, they sat over the remnants of an exquisite chocolate dessert—one plate; two forks—laughing.

"I hate to cut this short," The Woman said, sounding truly regretful, "but I promised I'd at least make an appearance at the party my publisher's throwing."

Disappointment flashed across his face. "Do you have to?" he said, sounding equally regretful.

"It's tempting to punt, but I can't. I promised the author I was on the panel with today that I'd go. I specifically don't want to let her down."

"And *that's* why I want you to become *my* editor." No longer disappointed, now he looked inspired. "But here's a thought: Would you mind if I tag along? Perhaps you could even introduce me to your publisher? It would all be strictly professional." He paused, then flashed a brilliant smile. "I happen to love parties."

"That," The Woman said, meaning every word, "would be wonderful."

.   .   .

Oh no! was my first thought when The Woman finished speaking. *New Man loves parties? What worse quality could he possibly have?*

But just as soon as the panic set in, rapidly thwacking my tail against the floor, quickly, I told myself to cool my jets. It was just a work dinner. He was an author, she was now his editor, it was all just business.

Her friends had been hanging on every word as she spoke. I'd been hanging on every word too; so much hanging, I'd forgotten to go after the drips of nacho dip. Seeing the error of my ways, I quickly made up for lost time.

"Well," The Redhead from the Art Department said, "he sounds like a lot more fun than the last guy!"

I sneered quietly at this, getting riled up, feeling my hackles rise.

"The last guy"? She made it sound like they were nothing. They were together for three years! Plus . . .

The Man was plenty of fun! He loved to take long walks, he was great for cuddles on the couch, and he was never too tired to throw a ball or a Frisbee just one more time. Or a hundred. What more could anyone want from a guy? OK, so maybe some of his more sterling qualities weren't always discernible to other humans, but . . . The Man was plenty of fun!

Anyway, like I said, the stuff with New Man was just business. Even though they were officially broken up, I was sure The Woman wasn't looking to replace The Man romantically—they were meant for each other!

"But he's going to be my author," The Woman told The Redhead. Ex-actly.

"I can't date my author," The Woman said, firm, decisive.

Before I could seek out more nacho dip drips, a resounding chorus rang out.

"You're right!" The Blonde said.

"Of course you can't!" The Redhead said.

"Of course you can!" said The Brunette from Accounting, who, if you asked me, should've just stuck to her numbers.

The others all stared at her, which, from The Blonde, was more of a glare.

"What?" The Brunette said. "Oh, come on. Yeah, I get it: Me Too and all of that. But it's not like the typical editor/author relationship with the editor being in a position of power over the author. *No* editor is in a position of power over an author who's *that* successful."

Still, the others stared and glared at her.

"What?" The Brunette said again. "Doesn't anyone else believe in true love? What if this guy turns out to be her soul mate? The love of her life? Should she ignore the possibility of true love just because of what others might think?"

Oh, I didn't like where this was going, at all.

I thumped my tail to express my displeasure, wishing they could hear the thoughts running through my mind:

No! No! Of course you can't! Think about the potential lawsuits!

"It's not like it's illegal," The Brunette muttered.

Damnit. Then how about ethics. Has anyone here ever heard about ethics? Well, think about—

"Well, it's all moot, since that is *not* going to happen," The Woman said firmly. "I know I started this all by saying I thought I met some-one, but now I don't know why I put it like that. It's strictly business, and it's going to stay that way." She paused. "So, who *has* read the book?"

Not me! I'm just here for the wine and conversation! I thought with a deep sense of relief. And I was relieved. Deeply. Because if The Woman was changing the subject back to the book that I was sure none of them had read, she wasn't serious. And if she wasn't serious, there was nothing for me to worry about.

"I have!" The Blonde said to The Woman. "I was fascinated by the symbolism in Marissa's character . . ."

Poseur, I thought with a yawn, as I settled back in over my front paws. *I bet you got that from reading Goodreads reviews.*

Still, while on the outside I may have looked yawningly nonchalant and all settled, on the inside my mind was racing.

And the dejected, distracted gaze on The Woman's face didn't help.

Chapter Sixteen

A few days later . . .

The Man had just popped the cap off a beer and I was eating a forgotten turkey chunk off the kitchen floor when a knock came at the door.

"*'Tis some visitor,*" I muttered, "*rapping at my chamber door . . .*"

Nah, I'm just funnin' ya. I'm not going to go all Poe on you here. I'm saving it. For Halloween.

The Man opened the door to reveal his editor: mid-forties, tweed jacket with elbow patches, horn-rimmed glasses, stiff as a board. If The Woman represents a more forward-thinking era in publishing, The Editor was decidedly old-school. Although, to my mind, while he might've *thought* he was a reincarnation of Maxwell Perkins, I'd say he was more on a level with . . . Well, I don't want to name any names. Let's just say that the real Max Perkins edited F. Scott Fitzgerald, including his masterpiece *The Great Gatsby*, which we all know I was named for. So I think I can say with more authority than anyone else, unless ol' Scott was still with us to say it himself: this guy was no Max Perkins.

I trotted over to stand beside The Man, in a show of solidarity, glaring up at The Editor. The Editor, in turn, glared back down at me. What can I say? I try to get on with people whenever I can, but even for me, it's just not always possible.

The Man stepped aside, gesturing with a magnanimous sweep of his beer bottle for The Editor to come inside.

Wait. We were inviting this guy *in*? I'd seen enough vampire movies—left running on the TV after The Woman had fallen asleep on the couch and The Man had escaped to another room, not that he'd ever admit he'd been scared—to know that once you do that, invite the vampire in, anything that happens afterward is on you.

"You know," The Editor said, with that ever-present condescending tone, which was one of the reasons I didn't care for him—like, get over your tweedy self, dude!—"if you'd agree to come to my office like a normal author, I wouldn't have to come down here."

See what I mean? The Man already knew he wasn't normal. There was no good reason to call attention to that fact.

"It could be worse," The Man said. "Stephen King used to make his editor and agent meet him at Red Sox games. Regularly."

"So you've said. Many times. I hate baseball."

"So you've said." The Man touched his backward Mets cap in acknowledgment. "Many times."

As they moved further into the apartment, The Editor abruptly shifted to, "I didn't want to do this over email, but—"

"Can I get you a drink?" The Man offered, cutting him off.

The Editor stared at the beer in The Man's hand, pointedly. "Do you have anything else?"

As a rule, The Man favors a good domestic beer. Further, he says that Budweiser will get you where you want to go just as quickly as anything else. But I guess that's not good enough for *some people*. Again, see what I mean? Accept the hospitality or don't accept the hospitality, but either way, there's no reason to be a tool about it. Do people still say "tool"? I don't know, but I saw it on an old show once and I liked it.

But, unlike me, The Man wasn't at all bothered by The Editor's blatant rudeness. I guess that, after all their years working together, he was used to it by then.

"Water," The Man replied with a shrug. "I got plenty of water."

"Fine," The Editor said with a sigh. "I'll take a beer."

Hey, don't do us any favors.

The Man disappeared into the kitchen. In his brief absence, I kept a wary eye on The Editor, who scowled back at me.

"I can't believe I'm going to drink a beer," The Editor muttered, "when I could be home enjoying dry martinis with my husband instead."

Wait. The Editor was gay? How did I not know this?

Reluctantly, I put a check in the positive column for The Editor, his first ever. I'm very pro-LGBTQ+.

Soon, The Man returned with fresh beers for each of them, and after delivering The Editor's to him, he plopped down in a chair. The Editor reluctantly took the chair beside him, back ramrod straight.

I guess The Man had finally decided to bite the bullet, because immediately, he opened with, "What didn't you want to do in an email?"

But before The Editor could answer, The Man continued with, "Let me guess: you didn't like the new book."

Still not waiting for an answer, The Man said, "And you didn't think it had enough heart."

"Wow," The Editor said, at last being given the chance to speak, "I guess I didn't have to come down here after all, since you knew exactly what I was going to say."

"Well," The Man said, "you could start by telling me what we do about it. What's next?"

"Look," The Editor said, "we all love you."

The Man did a not-so-subtle eye roll.

"OK, maybe that's too strong a word," The Editor said. "We all like you."

"You tolerate me."

"Yes." The Editor pointed his beer bottle at The Man in an uncharacteristically gauche gesture. "That." He paused, before adding with a rare and genuine enthusiasm, "But we love your writing! And we know what you're capable of. Because of that, we also know that this book is simply not the best you can do. And, I'm sorry to say, far from it."

The Man tilted his beer bottle, seeming to look to the familiar red-and-white label for inspiration, before taking a long swig. "I don't know how I'm supposed to write with a broken heart," he finally said.

"One would think that would fuel your writing—from great pain comes great art."

"One would think!" The Man barked a bitter laugh. "But no."

Over the course of this conversation, The Man had appeared to shrink in on himself, and as a result, I sharpened my glare on The Editor. OK, I may also have let out a growl. Just a tiny one.

"I have to say," The Editor said, uneasy, as well he should be, "your dog gives me the creeps."

"You're the only one who ever says that."

"Oh? Really? And how many other people come here?"

Silence from The Man accompanied by a glare at The Editor that was worthy of, well, me.

"That's what I thought," The Editor said.

"Other people come here," The Man said, now on the defensive, "sometimes!"

"Like who?"

"There was a delivery person here last week!"

Even I couldn't help but shake my head at the pathetic weakness of this response. If we're going to be loners, we should own it. Let's not pretend we're yukking it up with the Domino's kid on the regular. *Mmm, Domino's.*

"And her," The Man added softly, breaking my heart. "When she comes to pick up Gatz for the weekend, I still get to see her."

Wait. Was that an actual empathetic emotion I was seeing on The Editor's face? Was he feeling some small scintilla of . . . sympathy? Empathy? Some words have such a fine distinction, I can tell why some people confuse them.

"Maybe what you need," The Editor suggested, not unkindly for once, "is a change of scenery. Maybe"—and here his eyes lit up, like he was warming to his own idea—"you could get your creative mojo back if you took a vacation!"

The Man and I exchanged a look, then we both stared at The Editor.

Who did The Editor imagine he was talking to? A *vacation*? Had The Editor ever actually *met* The Man?

"Fine," The Editor said, mildly exasperated with us, and yet still curiously unwilling to relinquish hope. You know, that thing with feathers. "Then at least get out for a bit! What about meaningless affairs? That's what I always do when my heart is broken! Well, before I met the love of my life and got married." Wait. The Editor had a heart? Kidding! (Sort of.)

But seriously, what he'd said made me blink in shock, because it seemed to me that—against all odds—maybe, just maybe this guy was onto something here.

"I tried that already," The Man said. "It made things worse with . . . you know who, when she found out on Valentine's Day."

"Stop thinking about her!" The Editor said.

"The meaningless affair didn't go anywhere anyway," The Man said. "I broke it off right after Valentine's Day. She wasn't that interesting. She wasn't well-read. She hadn't even read *Othello*. Who hasn't read *Othello*?"

"I bet he hasn't," The Editor said with a rude chin nod at me.

Don't be too sure of that.

"Don't be too sure of that," The Man said, providing yet another reason for why I loved him so much. "Anyway, I just can't be with anyone who doesn't—"

"Stop thinking like you need to jump into another serious relationship!" The Editor cut him off. "You think *she's* doing that? No, *she's* living her best life with hot, poorly read, shirtless men on yachts. I'm almost sure of it. So get out there. Forget about her."

Meaningless affairs . . . Hmm . . .

"You know," The Editor said, thoughtfully studying the label on his own beer bottle, "this could be worse."

The Man waited, no doubt desperate to be happy again, practically on the edge of his seat, for The Editor's next words of wisdom. And I must confess that, for once, I waited on the edge of my seat too. For the first time in our long acquaintance it had occurred to me that this guy might actually know a thing or two.

"This," The Editor finally said, "could be a can."

Chapter Seventeen

Later the same evening...

A man and a dog walk into a bar . . .

It's good to have a place where everyone knows your name. I know this for a fact, because I saw it on the TV.

For us, that place had always been a local Irish pub, our neighborhood hangout, the only place outside of home and Nick's Italian Restaurant which The Man was ever reasonably comfortable enough to go to with any regularity. You know the kind of place I'm talking about: dartboard and a pool table and a few pinball machines, jukebox with no songs later than 1979, carpeting that had seen better days where there was more actual carpet and less floor showing through the remaining threads, the chief thing of beauty being a long mahogany bar running the length, at one end of which you can find the regular drunk old guy, while at the other is located the regular blowsy overage hooker. The kind of place where tourists wouldn't be caught dead but where, yes, really, everyone knows your name.

"Gatz!" The cry came at us from most of the assembly—because when I said "everyone," it was a slight exaggeration; some were complete strangers—as we filled the doorway. The place was reasonably packed, but as The Man and I—he in his disheveled best; me in the resplendent glory that is always me—made our way toward the bar, it was as though two stools magically appeared for us, side by side. The Man took the one on the left as I hopped up on the stool to his right.

The Bartender—early thirties, easygoing enough, tats up the wazoo—came right over with a bottle of Bud for The Man. Then he turned to me.

"What'll it be?" The Bartender asked.

I gave him my patented doggy equivalent of an eye roll.

The Bartender turned away. Returning a moment later with a large, hand-painted ceramic water bowl, he positioned it so I could see emblazoned across the front: *GATZ*.

I tell ya, it gets me every time.

"Let me know if you guys need anything else, all right?" The Bartender said, rapping his tatted knuckles on the bar twice before moving away to help another happy customer.

"Thanks, man," The Man called after him.

Another thing I've always appreciated about The Man? Even when the chips are down, he's always got manners.

The Man and I conferred with our beverages of choice, sipping and lapping respectively. Then, as one, we swiveled one hundred and eighty degrees on our stools to survey the room. The Man moved to nonchalantly rest both elbows on the bar behind us, looking awkward for just a brief moment as one elbow missed. I would've tried to mirror the double-elbow maneuver, but I like to think I know my limitations. And anyway, on me, I thought the move would look kind of douchey.

Keeping both eyes on the room, The Man leaned in my direction, coming in for a whispered conference.

"What do you think?" he said. "See any good meaningless-affair prospects?"

He may have seemed smooth to the point of oiliness, like this was no big deal to him and he was just some regular sleazeball, but his jangling nerves were highly palpable to me, and I could see his hand shaking as he death-gripped his beer.

Dude, no one's going to be able to hold your beer if you hold it that tightly!

I scanned the room. There were plenty of women in sight, in all shapes, ages, and sizes. There was even quite an array of dispositions on display, from the fun-loving to the crying-in-your-Chardonnay type. I'm as empathetic as the next dog, but to me, the crier was a nonstarter; we were depressed enough in our household already. And the angry one? Don't get me started. That woman was just frightening.

For the next half hour, I indicated prospect after prospect with juts of my chin. And, for the next half hour, I watched The Man strike out, time and time again.

Geez, he wasn't very good at this.

"This isn't as easy as it looks on TV," The Man observed.

Nothing ever is, pal. Nothing ever is.

But then my eyes at last located the best-looking woman in the room. No real intelligent spark in her eyes, so I had the feeling we wouldn't be talking Kafka, but she seemed neither depressed nor scary. I liked the shade of blue of the frilly scarf wrapped around her neck, and I nodded my snout in her direction.

Hey, I figured, just because the interaction was supposed to be meaningless, it didn't mean she couldn't be a looker! And if he was only going to strike out again, then why not do it with the best-looking woman there?

Following the lead of my snout, The Man took a deep breath and was half up from his stool when the good-looking woman caught sight of us. And then a curious thing happened. She eagerly made a beeline in our direction.

"Oh my god," she exclaimed, "your dog is so cute!"

There was that word again. I wanted to growl my displeasure at her lack of originality, but, what the heck? I was cute, she was cute, in that moment we were all cute.

"That's funny," The Man said, taking a blind stab at being suave and *almost* hitting the mark, "Gatz was just telling me he thinks you're cute too."

"I'm flattered," she said, hand to scarf accompanied by a modest smile. "To think that I caught the attention of the famous Gatz."

Huh, it occurred to me for the first time. *I guess I am famous.* Pause. *Well, in here.*

"Apparently," she went on, "everyone in here loves Gatz."

"Well," The Man said, without a trace of envy, "Gatz does have that effect on people."

"And is Gatz available?" she asked, now scratching me behind the ears, which I accepted gratefully. "It's so hard to meet an available man in the city."

She may have been acting like she was talking about me, but somehow, I sensed that her attention had shifted.

"Well," The Man said, "he might be available for some things."

"So," she said, "what do you do?"

"Well," The Man started, and it occurred to me that he'd started three consecutive sentences with the word *Well*. Couldn't he come up with something more original? Maybe add a little variety? Synonyms for "well" are hard to come by in this context, but he could at least try. He was supposed to be a writer, for gosh sake, a literary writer! "He's a dog, he eats a lot of treats . . ."

Heh. OK, that was a bit better. Pretty funny stuff.

Apparently, she thought so too, because she laughed before asking, "No, what do *you* do?"

"Oh, I'm a writer. The dog's not a writer. That would be pretty ridiculous if I said that, wouldn't it?"

Hey, now!

"Although I suspect," The Man went on, "if Gatz *were* somehow to write a book, he'd be better at it than I am."

That was better.

"But no," The Man went on some more, "the dog isn't the writer. The dog likes treats and I'm the writer."

And now, having witnessed it for myself, there was absolutely no doubt in my mind why The Man kept striking out.

"You mean like a *published* writer?"

"As opposed to the unpublished kind?"

She nodded.

"That would have to be a yes then. I write novels."

Her eyes lit up, not the first time I'd seen a relative stranger react this way. Almost everyone wants to be a writer. And when they meet someone who actually is, some of them go kind of gaga. Like: "Can you tell me how to get published?" or "I have this idea for a book—maybe you'd like to write it with me?" Stuff like that.

"How cool is that!" she said.

Inwardly, I had to agree. The Man and I were impressive in our accomplishments.

"I'd love to read a book someday," she added enthusiastically, "if I ever have the time."

Oh brother. See what I meant about the Kafka? There are three categories of humans: people who read books, people who write books, and then there's everybody else. Still, when it comes to meaningless, it doesn't get any better than that. We were in!

Chapter Eighteen

The following Friday evening . . .

I was lying on the couch, chewing on The Good-Looking Woman's scarf, which she'd left behind. Hey, what can I say? Some people are always losing stuff. Or maybe she was looking for an excuse to come back. Suddenly, there was a knock at the door.

The Man came out of the kitchen to answer it. It was The Woman.

"Hi," The Man said somberly.

"Hi," The Woman said, just as somber.

Ever since their big breakup, this was what things had been like between them whenever they'd meet: a world filled with somber.

But I didn't have time to dwell on the sadness of the human condition, because it immediately occurred to me that I needed to hide that stranger's scarf. I'd already screwed up once with those Valentine's Day chocolates. I wasn't about to make the same mistake twice with some attractive piece of neckwear. Live and learn, I always say, or learn nothing and stay stupid. Hurriedly, I desperately nosed the scarf down between the couch cushions before bounding to the door, eager to greet her.

"Gatz!" The Woman cried, dropping to my side to exchange affections.

For my part, I rolled onto my back and assumed the position.

A rub here; a scratch there. I looked up just in time to catch The Man gazing down at us wistfully.

The Woman rose to her feet.

"So," she said, "I'll bring him back Sunday night. I might be a little late. I hope that's OK."

"Sure," The Man said. "I'll be here."

She nodded knowingly. I did as well. Where else would The Man be?

Ask her in! my mind screamed, as I barked encouragingly at him. *Offer her a drink!*

But he didn't.

"OK, then," The Woman said.

If you asked her in, she'd come in! my mind screamed some more, as I figure-eighted my way in and out of their legs, hoping to nudge them closer together.

"OK, then," The Man said.

The Man nodded as she and I walked out the door, his hand on the knob, preparing to close it behind us.

Outside, on the steps of the brownstone, The Woman paused to zip up her raincoat. There seemed to be the beginning of a storm brewing in the air.

I gotta tell you: it's hard being the product of a broken union. You love the one you're with . . . but you're always missing the one you're without.

Chapter Nineteen

The following night . . .

A man goes on a journey; a stranger comes to town. Some people claim that every story boils down to one of those two things. I'm no literary expert, although I do split my time between a writer and an editor, but to me they seem somehow like one and the same. And for either or both to occur, it involves someone coming in or out of a doorway, real or metaphorical.

This is all by way of saying—albeit in an artsy-fartsy way—that it had seemed to me, lately, that a lot of my life was governed by knocks at the door, to wit:

"I'm so glad you could make it!" The Woman enthused, opening the door, following the knock.

I stood faithfully by her side, taking in the sight of the preposterously handsome man standing there: outside of the tiny scar under one eye, he really was Henry Golding to a T. I'd heard about this guy.

Apparently, New Man had come to call.

You'd think she might have warned me or something.

Unprepared as I was, he was a lot to take in.

New Man had a James Bond type of raincoat, damp spots sprinkled on his shoulders—it had been that kind of early spring—with a bottle in each hand.

I have to confess, I couldn't stop gawking. Damn, he was handsome, like . . . damn handsome. He *almost* made *me* look like chopped liver!

"Can I take your coat?" she offered.

Deftly, like if he had a third bottle he could easily do a juggling trick with them, he transferred one bottle to the other hand—so the guy was holding two bottles in a single handsome hand!—while slinking his arm out of one sleeve and then just as deftly repeating his neat little maneuver on the other side.

Show-off.

She hung up his coat, and as they moved off toward the kitchen, I trotted behind, worried. He was so undeniably suave. He really could be the next James Bond!

"I wish we could have met at the office," The Woman said.

Phew! As soon as she mentioned her office, I knew what I was dealing with here: a work-related meeting over food. It wasn't something she did often, inviting authors over to discuss their work, but when the author lived in the city or close enough, it had been known to happen.

"And I'd have gladly come there," New Man said.

"But, as I explained, there's construction going on, so it's been too noisy, and I've been working from home this week. And while a coffee shop or restaurant would have been more neutral territory, I thought we might get interrupted by your fans."

"That's not something that happens," he said with a self-deprecating smile.

Ah, crap. He even did self-deprecating well, which is not an easy thing to do.

"I was joking about the fans." She laughed. "But while it's fine to write in a coffee shop, it's tough to discuss a manuscript with all that noise going on."

"So we're here," he said simply.

"We're here," she agreed. Suddenly, she noticed that he was still holding his two bottles. "Oh! Let me . . ."

"Oh!" he said at the same time, like he'd also suddenly remembered he was still holding two bottles. "I got one of each, a red and a white, since I didn't know what we'd be having."

One of each? Sheesh. What a try-hard. Some people would just bring a six-pack of Bud and call it good enough, and I would agree with those people.

"How thoughtful!" she said. Then she added more soberly, "Although I'm not sure we should be drinking wine at a business meeting." And then: "Still, either is perfect because I made—ta-da!— takeout." She gestured at the little cartons of Chinese dotting the counter space; huh, I'd thought those were just for us. "I was going to make something impressive, but I got so caught up in rereading your manuscript, the day simply got away from me."

I wondered if New Man was experiencing the conversational whiplash that I was. She was appreciative of the wine, then admonitory, then appreciative again. She emphasized it being just business, then she talked about having thought of making something impressive. It was like listening to a human yo-yo. Did *she* even know what she wanted? Did *she* even know what this was?

"That's OK," New Man said. "If you'd made something impressive, I'd have had to make something even more impressive to reciprocate. This way, I only have to get more impressive takeout."

I didn't want to see what I was seeing, but I couldn't help it. There was an undeniable spark of . . . *something* between them as they maneuvered around each other in her kitchen: her pointing out where various things were stored, him passing her stuff, them accidentally brushing shoulders and laughing about it as they served themselves.

But no. This couldn't be meaningful interaction I was seeing. It had to be meaningless. I was sure of it.

Still . . .

Reciprocate? I began to panic. *Sure, reciprocation is a hallmark of good manners—and I'm almost always in favor of good manners, but please don't reciprocate! And don't try to be more impressive—you're already way too impressive as it is!*

But wait. Why was I getting myself so worked up about this? Normally, they'd have met at the office, and they were simply meeting here because of the construction and also like she'd occasionally done with other authors in the past, indicating that this was just a working dinner. This was *just* a working dinner . . . right?

They brought their wineglasses and plates to the table, settled down, and much to my relief, it really was all business.

"I love everything about the manuscript," she said with an enthusiasm that was just shy of gushing. "It's witty, insightful, and not in that know-it-all way some authors have that readers can find so offputting . . ."

"But . . ."

"But?"

"There's always at least one but, if not a hundred," New Man said good-naturedly. This was a little bit surprising, because usually when The Man's editor brought up his buts, The Man had a tendency to bristle defensively even if it was just one. This guy, on the other hand, seemed to welcome it, as evidenced by his adding, "And whatever yours are, I'd love to hear them. I don't want to be told anymore that something's fine when it could be better."

"OK, but—" she started to say and then she laughed and he laughed at her so quickly using a dreaded "but."

"Well," she said, still smiling, "I did have a few ideas. Perhaps it would be easier if I . . ."

She moved to the coffee table to grab her laptop. I watched her go with admiration, and then I watched New Man watch her with admiration. It was all very unsettling.

But as he moved plates and things out of the way to make room for her laptop, and as she sat down and they both settled into the business of her showing him what sort of editorial changes she had in mind, it really was all business.

Time passed.

Work continued.

My attentive vigilance began to wander.

Hey, you try listening to two people go on and on about plot, theme, tropes, story arc, character consistency, and continuity issues, not to mention the occasional subject-verb disagreement—all about a book you haven't had the pleasure of reading—and let's see how long you stick with it!

Before long, I was nosing among the cartons for leftovers.

Before much longer than that, fueled by MSG-infused moo shu pork, I was chasing my own tail around for amusement.

And before too much longer than *that*, I felt myself beginning to drowse on the sofa, not too far from where they still worked. My eyelids grew heavy, the god of sleep Hypnos carrying me away on Lethe, the river of forgetfulness and oblivion.

It was something of a surprise, then, to wake to a palpable shift in the atmosphere.

Gosh, I thought, shaking my head to clear out the cobwebs, *I hope I wasn't snoring out loud.*

The lights had been dimmed, and there were sounds in the air that could only be described as . . . *mood music.*

Oh no! Immediately, I was fully awake and fully anxious too. What was going on here?

Maybe it doesn't mean anything, I told myself. But then . . .

Oh hell. Romantic music and soft lighting ALWAYS means something! How did we get from mixed metaphors and scene continuity to THIS?

Quickly, I sprang into action.

Shakespeare would have advised: first, kill all the lawyers. Me, I could only go with one of my biggest strengths.

First, I barked.

And when that didn't garner the reaction I was looking for—or, really, any reaction at all—I went full-on ballistic: barking my fool head off and tearing around the place in my search for them until I finally found them in the kitchen, talking over yet more glasses of wine; I could tell it was "more" because the color of this wine was different than the color of their dinnertime wine. You'd think that with the racket I'd been making, they'd have heard me coming and been alerted to my impending presence, but as I barreled into the room, my nails sliding on the linoleum, New Man startled, taking an awkward little hop backward. It was weird, because The Man did awkward on the regular, and I was used to it, but on this guy it looked super strange; like he did awkward so rarely, he was awkward at it. Still, even The Woman seemed to be caught off guard.

"Oh!" The Woman said. "I forgot to take him out."

Him? *Him?* Now I was just a *him?*

"Would you like to come with?" she offered New Man.

Hey, hold on here. We're consulting New Man about what he wants? What about what I want?

As The Woman got up and set her now-empty glass on the counter by the sink, New Man glanced warily my way. I, in turn, gave him good cause for that wariness by glaring back at him as I barked violently.

"Easy, Gatz," The Woman said. "We're going out."

"I, uh, I think I'll stay here," New Man said.

"No problem." The Woman shrugged. "We'll be back in a few minutes. Let me just grab my coat, Gatz."

As she exited the room, I backed toward the door, keeping my eyes on New Man all the while.

That's right, pal. You better stay there.

He tried to break eye contact from my steely gaze, but I held firm.

When I heard The Woman call, "I'm ready now, Gatz!" from the general direction of the front door, I at last turned tail and trotted after her.

Once we were outside, a light drizzle falling upon us, I sulked as I walked beside her, barking loudly at the occasional passing truck.

Damn semis. Usually so much more sensitive to my every mood—which, I have to admit, is usually positive and upbeat—for once, she seemed completely oblivious.

"Oh, he seems so nice!" she said. "What do you think? Doesn't he seem nice?"

He's only "nice" if you like try-hards. He doesn't seem very nice to me.

"And smart. He's so smart!"

The Man's smarter. I'm almost sure of it.

"And he takes editorial direction so well!"

Well, I had to grudgingly admit, that part was true enough. When it came to editorial direction, The Man sucked. He fought back on *everything.* Even if the issue was as seemingly minor as a comma versus a semicolon, if he was forced to concede the battle, he'd be depressed for days afterward. I once heard The Editor tell The Man that if he weren't so brilliant, he'd tell him to take his Oxford comma and fuck off. In my experience, and in this one regard, most writers sucked. And yet I'd heard New Man accept all her suggestions with a calm equanimity; an eagerness, even.

"And he's, well, he's handsome, so handsome . . ."

Yeah, I guess. If you like that kinda thing.

"Not that that's the most important thing in the world."

It absolutely is not.

"But I can't get involved with one of my authors."

Of course you can't. That'd be ludicrous.

"Even though at least *one* of my colleagues says it wouldn't be unethical, because it's impossible for an editor to take advantage of an author of his stature."

Damn Brunette.

Normally, I prefer not to swear very much, even if it's just the word *damn.* I figure you can always come up with more original wording. But on that night, I was so worked up, the situation had me doing it on the regular.

"But it would still be unethical, because while it wouldn't be an abuse of power, it *would* be a conflict of interest. So I just can't."

Phew.

She sighed a heavy sigh, clearly disappointed.

"Aren't you gonna go, buddy?"

Oops, guess I didn't need to go for a walk after all.

Returning to the apartment a few minutes later, it immediately became apparent that, in the short time we'd been gone, New Man had taken it upon himself to tidy up. The dishes had been brought from the dining area into the kitchen, and we found him washing the last of them, a towel jauntily tossed over one shoulder.

What a try-hard. Also? I hate jaunty. Unless I'm the one doing it.

On the plus side, the music had been turned off and the lights were now fully on. The mood had been broken.

Thank the Universe.

Seeing her come in, New Man wiped his hands on the towel.

"I had a really great time tonight," he said.

How original. And she thought this guy was so smart?

"I did too," The Woman said. "The work went very well," she added stiffly.

"You're every bit as wonderful an editor as I thought you'd be when I met you at the London Book Fair."

I couldn't deny what I was seeing. Clearly, she was pleased with his words.

"Thank you. It's easy with a writer like you."

Words, schmords, I tried to dismiss in my mind. *Any idiot, any schmo can string together a few pleasing words.*

Dismissive as I sought to be, I was increasingly concerned, filled with the hopelessness, however trite the metaphor, of watching a train crash.

"The renovations on the office should be done next week," The Woman said, "so we should start meeting there."

"To work on the book," New Man said, somehow sounding disappointed.

"To work on the book," she said firmly.

Like a moment of zen or that one time I tried doggy yoga, I felt my whole being relax.

Yes. Smarter heads were prevailing here.

No matter what the contents of their words, though, I sensed a mutual feeling on both sides. And if I had to put a word to it, that word would be . . . *longing*.

Unlike with The Man and his quest for meaningless affairs, New Man—even if, so far, it had all been just "business"—seemed like a genuine threat to my ultimate goal: getting The Man and The Woman back together.

"Well," New Man said, visibly perking up a bit, "I'm just grateful to have you as my editor. I love working with you."

"And I feel the same," she said.

I could tell she meant it. There's probably little more gratifying for an editor than a writer who takes direction well, so of course she'd like his company.

"Maybe," New Man said, then hesitated.

"Maybe?"

"Maybe," he tried again, obviously nervous, "maybe when editing is over, I could take you out for coffee . . ."

"Maybe you could," The Woman said, cautiously, before adding a firm: "But only after editing the book is completely finished."

"Then here's to quick editing," New Man said.

Once New Man was safely on the other side of the front door, I slumped to the floor in post-anxiety exhaustion. Gosh, this was depressing.

I felt a familiar tug on my bladder.

Oh great. Now I really did have to go for a walk.

Chapter Twenty

The next afternoon . . .

Doors! Doors! Too many f-ing doors!

The Man and The Woman were standing inside of his front door, The Woman having just dropped me off at the end of the weekend. On our walk over there, the rain had finally stopped, but the weather was still moody, as the tail end of March is wont to be.

So, yeah, we were standing in a doorway again, but this time, unlike at the commencement of the weekend, when The Woman had looked sad and wistful, now she looked like something resembling content. I hadn't missed the change, and The Man, while never a great one with the old social cues, couldn't help but note it too.

"Wow," he commented, "you look so much happier than the last time you were here."

"That was just two days ago," she pointed out.

"Still." He paused. "Have you . . . *met* someone?"

That was quite a leap for anyone to make and especially for someone who missed social cues on the regular, but he did know her.

No! It was just a business dinner! How could she meet someone? You're The Man! You're THE Man!

"Maybe." She paused. "I don't know." Pause. "It's too early to tell." Longer pause. "It's complicated." Ridiculously long pause. "Why? Should I *not* meet someone?"

Maybe these two crazy kids couldn't see it, but I could see it: there was still a spark between them, however small. All he had to do was say, *No, you shouldn't, because I want to try again, but it won't be the same as before, it'll be better, I'll be better.* All he had to do was say it like that, in that awkwardly hurried way he could have sometimes—like how, even though he was this brilliant writer, on paper, when he tried to say important things out loud they came out jumbled like he was verbally illiterate—that I knew she once found so charming and still could again, and she'd say yes. She'd give it another go. I was sure of it.

I thumped my tail to try to get their attention as I tried to telepathically transmit my thoughts to The Woman: *You shouldn't! You shouldn't ever meet anyone ever! Not unless it's to have a meaningless affair! MEANING-LESS good! MEANING-FUL NO!*

But it was all to no avail. No one could hear my silent screams. Or my soft whining. For once, no one even paid heed to my thumping tail, too caught up were they in their human determination to screw everything up.

"No, of course you should," The Man said. "I mean, we're not together anymore . . . right?"

But you should be! You should be together! The three of us should be together forever and ever!

"Right," The Woman said.

NO!

Chapter Twenty-One

The same afternoon . . .

The Woman had looked a little less sparkly as she left.

The Man had looked even sadder than usual.

Me, I knew what I had to do.

I leaped a few times until I caught the sleeve of The Man's windbreaker in my mouth, tugging it down from the coatrack, and looked up at him. He nodded down at me.

Sometimes, a guy's just got to get out of the house to beat the ol' depression, before he goes mad.

I figured we'd go to the park. Is there any better cure for depression than the park? The smells of nature, so much nicer than exhaust fumes. The sounds of children laughing. The breeze ruffling my fur as I chased after a stick.

But The Man had other ideas.

"How about the bookstore?" he said.

Oh, that never helps! You'll get more depressed there. You'll be annoyed there aren't more of your books on the shelves or more copies of the books that are there. You'll be annoyed that the ones that are there are displayed spine out as opposed to the far more preferable face out. Then you'll rail against the literary establishment. Happens every time.

Still, I have an optimistic nature. So while I'm familiar with the theorem that states that doing the same thing over and over while expecting a different result is the definition of insanity, I have a different take: Why not hold on to hope? Why not hope that things and people *can* be different? That's not insanity, my friends. That's *optimism*.

So I maintained my optimism as we walked into the bookstore. Plus, I've seen all the same rom-coms everyone else has. I *know* bookstores are considered to be a primo place for a meet-cute. And while we weren't looking for romance, it could at least be a better-lit and therefore less-depressing locale than the watering hole for picking up chicks.

I maintained that optimism as we passed by the front tables with their endless selections. Sometimes, it feels like there are *too* many selections. I always think that if *I* owned a bookstore, it'd just contain endless shelves of the greatest novel ever written, *The Great Gatsby*. That, and The Man's books, of course.

And I maintained that optimism as we passed by several prospects on our way to the place in the alphabet where The Man's books are shelved and held on to a tattered shred of it right until the moment the manager caught The Man moving his books to a more prominent place, asked The Man what he thought he was doing, The Man railed against the literary establishment, and we left in disgrace.

I worried, then, that we'd just go back to the apartment.

But The Man surprised me.

See what I'm talking about? Live in hope. Be aware that you might not get a different result. But live in hope.

"How about the park, Gatz?" he suggested. "It's where we should've gone in the first place."

The park! YES! He was right! And yes, we *should* have gone there in the first place!

OK, here's something I don't know how to verbally categorize. If insanity is supposed to be that other thing, what do you call it when you do a thing you always do and you *don't* get the expected result?

What I'm trying to say is that on that day, for the first time in the history of the Universe, the park let me down.

Everywhere we looked, humans of all ages, shapes, and sizes were paired off, holding hands. Romance was in the air, far as our eyes could see. I guess springtime in the city can have that effect on people. But did they all have to be doing it? Did there have to be so much PDA? Did they all have to be so obviously in love? I felt like we were being assaulted . . . by romance!

"Is it just me, Gatz," The Man said, "or is this even more depressing than the bookstore?"

It's not just you, pal. And please, don't even think about throwing a stick for me. Sure, I'll chase after it, because I'll have to, but it won't be any fun. Not really.

Sometimes, The Man can read me like a book, because he did not pick up any sticks to throw.

"Should we just go for a drink?" he suggested instead.

Which was how we found ourselves back at our neighborhood watering hole.

We surveyed the options together, and I started to nudge him in one direction, when The Man stopped me, looking completely the other way.

"I got it this time, buddy," he said.

He seemed strangely confident, so unlike his usual self. But then it occurred to me: After the debacle at the bookstore and the fiasco at the park, maybe he felt like he had nothing left to lose? People with nothing left to lose are always strangely confident, at least in my experience.

So, I watched The Man go off to a different lady, who seemed to get a kick out of all of his awkward motions. Dejected, I slumped my snout down against the bar. I saw The Man point across the bar and the lady he was talking to give me a nod.

"Can I get you a drink?" my tatted bartender pal offered.

I wondered: Did I want a drink? Did I really want to accept sustenance, carrying on in a world in which love didn't work like it should? Maybe I should just let myself waste away and . . .

Oh hell. There was no need to get extreme about it.

Still dejected, however, I managed a weak nod.

My special bowl appeared before me, and I lapped at the water, all the while thinking: *I don't understand how he thinks he can do this without me. Doesn't he know I'm the greatest wingdog ever? How can he do anything but strike out without me?*

I looked down and saw the bowl was empty.

Huh. How did that happen?

I looked up at The Bartender.

"Hit you again, buddy?" he offered.

I woofed and watched as he topped me up.

And hey, don't call me buddy, buddy. Only The Man and The Woman get to do that!

Across the bar, I could see that The Man and the lady he'd picked for himself—let's just call her Bar Woman—were playing darts. Since this was an activity I'd never seen him engage in before—the bar previously being a place we came to in order to take a break from writing and the tyranny of the blank page, except that last time when we came to pick up a chick—I hopped off my stool and trotted over to check out the action and maybe see if he needed my help.

Bar Woman only gave me a perfunctory greeting. It was polite enough but by no means the usual gushing I was accustomed to. But that was OK. In my current state, I wasn't in a mood to be gushed at. As for The Man, he appeared to be doing all right for himself, even without my assistance.

Oh, not at the darts. It soon became apparent that he sucked at darts.

Bar Woman hit a bull's-eye. The Man tossed his dart, and it hit the wall, barely missing the Miller High Life clock. Well, at least he almost hit something.

Bar Woman laughed good-naturedly.

See what I mean about him doing all right for himself? Even without my help, he was garnering a good-natured response.

"You're not so good at this, are you?" Bar Woman observed, not unkindly.

"It might not be my game," The Man allowed.

Well, that was obvious.

Soon, Bar Woman had cleaned his clock and they were off to the pool table for what she referred to as "a game of stick." Not my idea of a game of stick, for sure—no one even threw anything—but hey, I get it. Not everything is about me.

From what I could gather, they were playing solids against stripes. And before I knew it, there were only a few solids left, while all the stripes remained.

Bar Woman sized up a shot, tapped her stick against three different banks, bent over the table, and took aim. I gotta admit, she came close to pulling it off, but no cigar.

Yes! Now, The Man would stage an impressive comeback. I was sure of it.

The Man leaned over the pool table with his own stick, only knocking some of the balls slightly out of position with his elbow. He looked up at her apologetically, but she waved a dismissive hand. Even though his unintentional jostling had caused some of his own balls to be more fortuitously situated near pockets, she didn't appear to be bothered by that fact. This, to me, seemed to be a mark in her favor, since I tend to detest sticklers, unless I'm the one doing the stickling.

The Man went back to his shot, focusing all his attention on propelling the white ball into his stripe, hit the cue ball, and . . . it popped up and sailed right off the table.

"You're not so good at this either," Bar Woman observed, still good-naturedly; maybe even more good-naturedly.

"Can't say that I am," The Man admitted, clearly not bothered, which was strange. The Man usually hated being bad at things and especially hated having other people see him being bad at things.

From darts to pool to the ancient pinball machines. No Black Panther or Wonder Woman for this joint, no sirree. It was Mata Hari,

Space Shuttle, Playboy (like the bunny), and Kiss, like the rock band with all the makeup and the giant tongue hanging out.

She chose Kiss.

Well, who can blame her? I thought, distractedly sniffing the butt of another dog on the premises. The Playboy one looked so sexist to me. I know sometimes I refer to women as chicks and I encourage The Man to have meaningless affairs, but that's just me getting my macho on and trying to be helpful. But come on. I do have my standards.

Bar Woman proved to be as adept at pinball as she had been at darts and pool. Before I knew it, having been too distracted by dog butt to pay much attention, she had a high score on the machine—high score!—and she was only on her first ball.

When that ball finally guttered down the side, she hit at the flippers like she could make it unhappen, yelling at the machine.

Wow, some people are competitive.

Realizing that hitting and yelling wasn't achieving the desired effect, Bar Woman gestured to The Man to take his turn.

The Man gamely bellied up to the machine, tugged on the knob, and then let go of it so that the spring coil could propel his little silver ball into the upper reaches of Kiss, where it completed a stunningly slow arc, occasionally pinging against a buzzer or two before falling down straight toward the center gap between the two flippers.

"You're supposed to . . ." Bar Woman started to say.

But there was no point, as The Man, with no effort to stop what was happening, watched the ball go right through.

"That's amazing," she said. "I didn't think it was humanly possible to get so few points out of a ball."

The Man shrugged, not bothered.

"Well, now you know," he said.

"You're not so good at . . . any of this," she said.

Again with the shrug. "I guess I'm not really a . . . bar game kinda guy."

"Is there anything you are good at?"

"Well, I'm told I'm a pretty good writer . . . and I have a few other talents . . ."

It's at this juncture that I should point out that between all the attempts at games, The Man had made regular forays to the bar to get them more drinks, and these were not his usual beers; these were real drink-drinks, with the hard stuff in them, which maybe explains why, at his mention of his "few other talents," she abruptly grabbed him by the lapels of his windbreaker, smashing her lips against his.

I'll say one thing about Bar Woman: everything she did, she did with great conviction.

As for The Man, he smashed his lips right back, even though conviction was much rarer for him, which is how we found ourselves stumbling out onto the sidewalk and then stumbling our way home, some of us stopping to smash-kiss along the way.

The two of them crashed into the apartment, no one even taking notice of me or the fact that my food bowl was perilously close to empty as they crashed their way across the floor and into the bedroom. As they crashed, I followed along as best I could, looping in and out of their legs. Bar Woman almost tripped at one point, but The Man quickly righted her, and soon they were smash-kissing some more on the side of the bed. But then . . .

You know how you can just sense it when someone is staring at you?

All of a sudden I noticed that, while still lip-locked with The Man and with one eye closed, Bar Woman had the other eye locked on me. It was like she couldn't take her eye off me, and not in a good way.

For my part, I suppose I was glaring at her from where I sat on my haunches, doing sentry duty from the doorway.

"Um," she said, unlocking her lips. "I hate to say it, but your dog is kinda freaking me out right now."

With a sigh, The Man made his way to the bedroom door.

"Sorry, Gatz," he said. "I guess not everyone likes an audience."

Then, gently, oh so gently and yet somehow still it hurt, The Man eased me out of the doorway, gave me a soft shove in the direction of the living room, and then quietly clicked the door shut behind me.

I suppose I could've remained just outside the door, listening in. But I knew what I'd hear: the mattress bouncing, sighs, and cries. Did I really need to hear all that? I did not.

I made my way to the couch, hopped up, and collapsed.

Not. Happy.

Sometime later, I roused to the sounds of people talking. Opening my eyes, I saw the early-morning light streaming into the room. Wow, where had the night gone?

I looked over to see The Man and Bar Woman standing near the front door. She looked pretty pleased with herself. He looked like, well, his usual awkward self. But it was a pleased awkward.

"I would do that again," Bar Woman said.

Immediately, The Man looked less pleased. "Uh . . . uh . . ."

Perhaps sensing his energy, as I was, she hastened to add, "Yeah, just so we're clear, I'm really more interested in *meaningless* right now. That is, assuming you are too."

The Man perked up at this, and I did too.

Now she was talking our language: *Meaningless is our middle name!*

"Meaningless would be ideal," The Man said with a relieved smile that I suppose she could've taken offense at but didn't.

"Great," she said. "Maybe I'll see you again then."

"Great."

She left, The Man shut the door behind her, and then he turned to me, eyes wide.

I could tell what he was thinking: Wow. She was going to maybe be a repeat offender!

Still, as I tried to be as excited as he was, feigning enthusiasm for his sake, my heart just wasn't in it.

Chapter Twenty-Two

Three weeks later . . .

It was the weekend, so I was, of course, with The Woman. And not only was it the weekend, it was also Book Club night, which is always exciting. And even more exciting than that, The Woman had told me there was going to be a special guest that evening.

I was beside myself with giddiness—The Man may not like to socialize, but I can be a total people dog when I let my inner social bee fly—but then the doorbell rang well before the appointed time and I saw that the "special guest" was New Man.

Oh joy.

Weren't these two supposed to be keeping it in the office until they finished editing his stupid book? Which would be, hopefully, never.

You'd think he'd sense my antipathy. And he seemed to, a bit. OK, maybe more than a bit, as he gave me a wide berth. But soon he was making himself at home in the kitchen as she calmly shuffled through her vinyls in the living room.

He was actually running himself quite ragged, which I was all for, calling out questions to The Woman, like "Which spoon goes with the salsa platter?" and "Where do you keep your cheese?"

I took particular exception to the latter question. The matter of where The Woman chooses to keep her cheese should be her business.

She seemed to answer all his stupid questions calmly, but I decided to trot over to the living room just to make sure. While tone of voice can be a great indicator of mood—certainly, The Man's said enough times that he wished he could read tone in emails and texts—there's nothing to replace seeing firsthand the accompanying facial expressions. I'd just bet she was rolling her eyes at his culinary ineptitude, like, *Wow, what a loser—that's the last time we invite him to Book Club!*

But when I joined her in the living room, I saw that . . .

Huh.

She didn't look turned off by the loser at all. On the contrary, she looked positively tickled.

"Where do you keep the fruit spoons?" New Man called out.

"Fruit spoons?" The Woman called back.

"You know. Spoons for fruit."

Her eyes twinkled some more as she placed an elegant hand over her mouth, apparently hoping to stifle a giggle and not being wholly successful at it. Then she rose to her feet and headed for the kitchen, presumably to put New Man out of his misery.

I tell you, I'd have liked to put him out of his misery . . . permanently and *not* metaphorically.

I trotted after her.

Once in the kitchen, she opened a drawer, removed a simple spoon, and extended it toward him.

"Here," she said, laughing, "is a spoon. I'm told it can even be used for fruit, making it, technically, for at least part-time in its life as a spoon, a fruit spoon."

New Man nodded, embarrassed.

"Right," New Man said, "right. Also . . ."

He moved a platter of tortilla chips from the counter to the island in the center of the room.

"Nachos?" he said, like nachos were some great sphinxlike "mysteries of the Universe" question just begging to be answered. "How do I make the nachos? Is there a certain way you'd like them made?"

"Well, I usually get some cheese. Toss it on. Melt it."

New Man nodded earnestly. "Hmm, very interesting. I hadn't thought of it that way before."

"I suppose," she said, "you could reverse it."

"Reverse it?"

"You know, melt the cheese first, then toss it on? But if you do that, you wind up with a cold chip. And who wants a cold chip in their nachos?"

"Right," he said, still earnest. "No cold chips here. Warm is good for nachos."

She laughed, smiling up at him, and immediately, the dead-earnest expression fell away. It was as though he could see for the first time that she'd been teasing him, maybe just a bit.

She looked up at him, eyes sparkling.

He looked down at her, eyes sparkling.

Thank *God* the doorbell rang right then!

That broke whatever spell had been between them, but just for good measure, I nudged my snout at the backs of her knees, propelling her toward the front door in order to let her guests in. Hey, it's not polite to keep people waiting!

"I'll be right there!" she called out.

"Melt the cheese, melt the cheese, *melt* the cheese," I heard New Man mutter to himself behind us, back to being earnest again.

Oh, forget that guy! I thought, actually able to do so, as I raced past The Woman in my eagerness. Did I mention how much I love Book Club? I bounded into the foyer, scratching at the door as The Woman reached from behind me to open it.

Sometimes, they arrive separately. But on this occasion, they all got there together.

The Blonde!

The Redhead!

The Brunette!

"Hi!" they all said at once.

"Hi! Welcome!" The Woman said back.

She greeted each of them as I curled my way through their legs, happily sticking my tongue out at her friends, who were my friends too. They, in turn, bent down to pet me, greeting me like I was the one they were there to see.

Which, on some level, you gotta admit, is probably true.

There were a lot of squeals of "Gatz!" as though it had been far longer than the few weeks since we'd seen one another. I guess some special beings always warrant a hero's welcome and I have always been one of those special beings.

But then into our happy grouping of four women loving on the Gatzer, he had to walk in and spoil it.

The smell was what alerted us to his presence first—the insanely beatific aroma of melted cheese, to be exact. Apparently, New Man had figured out the fine art of nacho making, and there he was, steaming platter in hand.

Who could resist?

It probably didn't hurt that, after they made their way into the living area and he gently set the platter down on the coffee table, he greeted each of them individually, like he was so happy to see them.

Well, who doesn't like a happy greeting?

It occurred to me for the first time that he actually must've met them all before this, during those times he visited The Woman at the office for things having to do with his book. But I supposed this was the first time they'd all been together in a more social setting, outside the office. And that if they'd been impressed with him before—all that "bestselling author" hoo-ha—they were even more impressed with him now, what with his kitchen towel draped casually over his shoulder and stuff.

Feh.

Anyone could feign being genuine, engaged, and kind for a little while. I seriously doubted he could pull it off for much longer, certainly not the whole night.

"Why don't we get started?" The Woman suggested.

"I have to say," The Redhead said, "my partner Mikaela is totally jealous of this evening. She considers herself to be one of your biggest fans."

More feh.

I dutifully parked myself in the corner, glaring surly eyes at New Man as he continued to impress The Woman's friends, offering the platter of nachos here and there before scurrying off to the kitchen, returning soon with a bunch of platters he juggled with ease.

You're really making yourself at home here, aren't you? I thought. *Well, I wouldn't let myself get too comfortable if I were you. But since I'm not you, I'm me, I'll make myself as comfortable as I damn please.*

New Man set his successfully juggled platters down on the coffee table, the eyes of the admiring group upon him.

Not my eyes, though. My eyes were not admiring in the least. I attempted to make my own version of a very familiar human gesture to illustrate this, pointing my paw at my eyes before turning the paw a one-eighty toward New Man—*I'm watching you, pal, at all times*—but for once, no one was paying any attention to me. Not even The Woman.

New Man took his spot in the middle of the couch, right between The Woman and The Blonde.

"So," The Woman said, clapping her hands together, a mischievous gleam in her eye, "who read the book this time?"

What was she talking about? Was there something different about "this time"?

All around the circle, there were excited affirmations and a lot of head nodding.

Huh.

I was an old Book Club hand, so I was well aware of the fact that, even when you're talking about a group of people who work in publishing—for joy, not glory—it's still rare when everyone's read the book.

But the reason for this soon became apparent.

"What a treat!" The Brunette gushed. "To have the author of the book we're discussing here! I mean, I know we've already met at the office . . ."

This was disappointing on more than one level. If they were talking about one of New Man's books, he'd be the focus of all their attention all night long. But also? I'd never known The Brunette to gush about anything before. Honestly, she just wasn't the gushing type. And yet, on she went, adding:

"And what a tall glass of water you are!"

And then, in a gesture I seriously hoped she'd look back on with great embarrassment when she rose the next day, she made a claw out of one hand, clawed at the air in his general direction, and let out a noise that sounded something like, "Mmmroar!"

New Man laughed along awkwardly, but not without kindness, although he did look a bit uncomfortable at being the focus of so much attention. Thankfully, The Blonde was having none of it. This was book-discussion time, and The Blonde, in my experience, takes her books seriously. Almost scarily so. *Almost* as seriously as she takes her wine.

"Although I'm usually more in favor of the reader-response school of lit crit," The Blonde began, "I'm sure we would all love to hear your personal insights." She leaned forward so far, in her effort to get at those insights, she almost fell out of her chair. "Could you talk a bit about your choice of thematic love and worship throughout the arc of the mail carrier? I don't want to be elitist, but I'd never before considered mail carriers to be tragically romantic heroes."

"But Anthony Trollope worked for the Post Office," The Woman pointed out. "You know? The author of *The Chronicles of Barsetshire*? And about a million other books."

New Man looked at her appreciatively.

"Gosh, yes," New Man agreed. "Trollope was insanely prolific. Do you know, he used to get up ridiculously early each morning and knock out thousands of words—thousands!—before heading out to his day job at the Post Office?" New Man shook his head in admiration. "I wish I could do that. Me, I'm a late-night writer by nature, which means I've had the whole day to let self-doubt creep in before sitting down to work. Although sometimes, I do the staring-at-the-blank-page thing for so long, it actually is ridiculously early the next morning before I hunt-and-peck out my first new words."

The assembly, except for me, pooh-poohed his modesty. They were all sure, even if I wasn't, that whenever he wrote he was brilliant.

"I suppose, though," New Man added, looking mildly embarrassed, "I should've bothered to reread my book, and I would've, had I known there'd be questions about theme and character arc."

"You can't remember your own book?" The Redhead asked.

"It has been a minute," New Man said. "It was my first, and sometimes, it feels like a different person wrote it—do you know what I mean?"

Maybe a different person did write it, I hoped. *Maybe he's one of these plagiarists you hear so much about, I'll find a way to expose him, and—*

"I completely understand," The Brunette said. "That's exactly how I feel every time I get a new pet snake."

The Woman and New Man made eye contact, bonding over the beautiful strangeness that has always been The Brunette.

"I buy them," The Brunette continued, "and they die and I buy them and they die. But you know? Every time I get a new pet, I feel closer to God."

Like a boa constrictor with a new mouse, they took a beat to digest this latest oddity.

"That's really beautiful," New Man observed at last.

I couldn't tell if he was sincere—I kinda hoped, for his sake, that he wasn't—but even I had to admit, it was a kind thing to say. He was making an effort to "meet someone where they are," as the saying goes.

I also had to admit that he probably wasn't a plagiarist. He probably simply meant to express something The Man was always saying: that for a writer to go back and read his or her earlier work, that way madness lies.

The Brunette blushed at New Man's remark. I rolled my eyes, just because. And The Blonde took a deep breath, no doubt gearing up to take another deep dive into New Man's debut novel from long ago.

The night went on, with New Man continuing to interact with each friend where they were.

They were all laughing; they were all charmed.

They, not I.

The Brunette was evincing a heretofore unseen side to her personality, a touchy-feely side that seemed to compel her to reach across and lay a hand on him somewhere, anywhere, whenever she was making a point.

The Redhead seemed the most overtly respectful, casting occasional looks The Woman's way, no doubt seeing the same thing I was seeing: that The Woman was content to simply sit back and watch the others talk to him.

Even The Blonde, who could be a handful in her own way, was won over as he hit all the right novelist beats for her, miraculously suddenly remembering his own work and reciting whole passages of it to her at her prompting.

Hell, he could even do accents well.

Anytime The Man read his own work out loud, when he got to a part where he'd need to voice a woman, he always flubbed it. The voice would always come out high and vaguely insulting. I knew he wasn't like that, that he didn't mean it that way. Some people just don't have a solid impersonation gene.

But this guy?

He raised his voice too, but he never went too high with it, so it never came off diminishing or condescending in any way.

But enough of that. The others were all content to compliment his strengths. I certainly didn't have to add to that chorus.

Not too long after they'd finished the most thorough examination of a book that Book Club had ever witnessed, The Brunette moved away from the group, dancing by herself in a chilled-out manner to the jazz music playing, a thankfully empty wineglass in her hand.

"You know," The Brunette said, "this is the best part of Book Club. I love the books—your book in particular is genius—but this is the best. We're analytical with books all day at work, you know? We rarely get to let loose like this!"

Dancing by yourself to softly playing jazz music didn't meet my personal definition of "letting loose"—which tended to involve flying objects and me running around like a furry little maniac—but hey, knock yourself out.

The Blonde clenched the stem of her wineglass, swearing under her breath, a tightening fist away from snapping it in anger.

"I swear to God," The Blonde said, "you push me to the edge."

Whoa, who lit her fire?

But here's the problem with The Blonde. Give her a third glass of wine or—perish the thought—a fourth, and you always run the risk that irrational anger will be the end result. And then, when that happens, look out, because—hoo-boy!—the non sequiturs really start to fly. Who knew what she meant by that last remark? In the moment, I wasn't sure she even did.

The Redhead gently pried the wineglass from her grip, and The Blonde immediately gave her a grateful smile that was a tad sheepish.

Hey, we all need to be cut off sometime.

You'd think New Man would be put off by all of this . . . strangeness. Certainly, it could get awkward the next time he saw them at the ol' office. And yet, he didn't seem put off by it at all, not any of it. On the contrary, he seemed as thoroughly charmed by The Woman's work friends as they were by him. And while I'd thought earlier in the evening that anyone could feign being genuine, engaged, and kind for a little while but that I seriously doubted he could pull it off for the whole night, here he was doing it. Could I have been wrong about him? Could he actually *be* genuine, engaged, and kind? Oh puh-leeze.

I shook my head at him, my glare intensifying into daggers.

At the very least, he could react like a normal person would. Couldn't he see how odd this group was?

Come on, pal—run for the hills!

But did he take my advice, delivered by mental telepathy?

No.

Instead, he started to stand, lifting an empty wine bottle off the coffee table.

"Why don't I grab another bottle?" he offered.

Before anyone could respond to this, The Blonde piped up again.

"Here's something I've been wondering," she said, and it was any-one's guess if she was feeling angry again or was simply being intense. "Is there any . . . *downside* to all this . . . *success?*"

New Man appeared to respectfully give the question careful thought before replying, "Well, there is that one stalker . . ."

"Wait," The Woman said. "You have a stalker? How did I not know about this?"

But before *that* could be explained, The Blonde dropped her wine-glass, and, well, you really can't leave wine all over the rug.

Paper towels were grabbed, cloth towels were grabbed, advice was shouted about the wonders of salt: not good for rubbing in wounds unless you're into S-M, but *great* for getting out wine stains.

After that was attended to, The Woman reached for the empty bottle New Man was still holding.

"You've already done so much," she said.

And that's when reaching turned to touching, her hand making physical contact with his, their eyes locking.

"I'll get it," she added, giving a slight tug on the bottle, the hand-to-hand contact thankfully separating once the bottle had wholly been transferred to her hand. Though I could've sworn I saw the lingering trail left by their parting fingers in the air, kind of like an LSD trail. Not that I do drugs. The Gatzer is firmly antidrug. But I'm no provincial. I know all about hallucinogens. I've seen *Go Ask Alice*. I've heard the Jefferson Airplane song.

New Man seemed to slightly blush as she maneuvered past him, his eyes watching her walk until she disappeared into the kitchen.

It struck me then that while New Man was all self-confident suaveness with the other three, The Woman made him nervous. It was like he cared what she thought.

The Brunette was too caught up in her jazzy dancing and The Blonde too caught up in her notes on the book to take notice of anything beyond "intellectual pursuits," but The Redhead saw what I was seeing, observing the sparky interaction between New Man and The Woman.

I always knew The Redhead was one sharp cookie.

The Redhead followed The Woman into the kitchen, and I hopped up, following The Redhead.

Hey, Redhead see, Gatz do.

The Redhead perched herself on the island, which I supposed was just barely OK since the food portion of the evening was finished, as The Woman played with the cork of a wine bottle, either not noticing or ignoring the way The Redhead was looking at her.

"What do you think of the new mail system at work?" The Woman said, finally breaking the silence.

"The new mail system?" The Redhead echoed, with a light mocking tone that could've easily made the leap across the aisle to scathing.

"Sure," The Woman said. "The reading has me thinking about the intensity of that civic duty. We can be so oblivious to the people who play essential roles in our lives—the man who runs the bodega, the conductor on the train, and, yes, the mail carrier—but when you think about it, really think, it's astounding that—"

"Are we really not going to talk about what happened out there?"

"What happened out where?"

When she'd spoken that last, The Woman met her eyes as the cork popped free. Then a smile spread across her face, almost involuntarily, it seemed, and she quickly returned her attention to the bottle.

"Come on," The Redhead said. "We're really not going to address the elephant in the room?" Pause. "Or should I say, the objectively handsome man in your living room?"

The corners of The Woman's smile spread even wider, if possible, as she kept her gaze downward. For my part, I continued looking anxiously between the two of them.

"Still not knowing what you're talking about here," The Woman said, suppressing the smile, trying to hide it.

"Don't be that way with me," The Redhead said. "I can see what you're like with him."

"I'm not any way with him," The Woman objected. But still, there was that smile. "He's my author."

"Our publishing house's author," The Redhead corrected. "And, oh, by the way . . . you so totally are!"

"So totally? What are we, twelve now?"

"Hey, don't knock twelve. When you're twelve, the world is still hopefully new and ideas are hopefully fresh."

"Be that as it may, and as romantic a notion of youth as it is, one I'm not sure I wholly agree with, there's still no need to—"

"You really like him!" The Redhead crowed.

"Shh!" The Woman shushed, warning finger to lips as she cast an anxious look between The Redhead and the doorway what with all it led to . . . beyond.

I gotta tell you, I was feeling anxious too, but my eyes were fixed in one place, squarely on The Woman.

"No, I don't," The Woman whispered, so low even I could barely hear her. "I can't."

But I could tell that the "don't" was a lie. Maybe she was even lying to herself about it, but it was still a lie.

I was crestfallen, for once struck mentally speechless.

Had I known this? Kinda? Sorta? It was one thing to kinda-sorta suspect a thing and quite another to have it confirmed during girl-to-girl talk.

"And even if I did, which I don't," The Woman said, "I can't do anything about it."

"Come on," The Redhead said. "You can find a way to work around this."

"No," The Woman insisted, "I really can't. I really like him, but I can't date him. It wouldn't be ethical. It wouldn't be right."

"But what if he turns out to be the love of your life? Does ethics demand you not explore the possibility with someone who could turn out to be the love of your life?"

Hey, now! That was The Brunette's line before! Whose side was The Redhead on here?

"I'm on the side of love," The Redhead said. "I'm always going to be on the side of love."

"Who said anything about love?" The Woman said. "I barely know him."

"And you should get to know him better," The Redhead insisted. "You owe it to yourself."

Just then, The Blonde sailed in, stopped, turned around, and sailed right back out again. Was she being socially sensitive? Was it that she noted that they were deep in private conversation? Was it because she was blazing drunk and forgot what she came in for in the first place?

"There's your answer," The Redhead said, indicating the space The Blonde had briefly occupied.

"I don't follow."

"She's not the editor you are, but she's still a decent editor."

I didn't entirely understand what The Redhead meant by this, but apparently The Woman got it.

"But I love working with him," The Woman objected.

"But you also don't feel like you can do both," The Redhead countered, "and I get it. So you have to choose. If she were to become his editor, your ethical dilemma would be solved."

"Maybe . . ."

"You'd probably still want to keep it on the down low for a while, but it's not like it would be forever," The Redhead went on. "I know we're fast-tracking his book. And you and he can always still talk about craft or whatever, but officially, she'd be his editor. Problem solved."

I gotta admit, I was a little confused at this point. She was his editor, she wouldn't be his editor, maybe she'd still be his editor? Honestly, it was all publishing to me.

The Woman cleared her throat, raised the bottle high, and sailed out to the living room.

"Who needs a top-up?" I heard her offer.

I hurried back to the living room, arriving just in time to see The Brunette thrust her empty glass forward.

"Yes, please and thank you," she said.

I watched New Man watching The Woman pour without her knowledge of his eyes or mine. In his now was a naked admiration. It was something I recognized because I shared that naked admiration. And you know who else shared it? The Man. The Man was the only non-canine allowed to admire her nakedly.

If I was mildly annoyed with this guy in the past, a little miffed maybe, now a fully formed anger was stewing inside.

But I had to, I knew, bide my time.

It was thus much later, the nacho platter vastly diminished, the group still laughing over their wine, when I saw my opportunity.

I'd been guarding the door, my eyes intently stabbing into New Man, who was starting to become aware of those stabs. Hastily, he got up, grabbing the platter.

"I'll go refill this," he offered.

Hey, hadn't he gotten the memo? The food portion of the evening was over, which was why it'd been OK for The Redhead to park her butt on the island.

Oh, wait. What was I objecting to? This was the moment I'd been waiting for.

"OK!" The Blonde said.

"Hurry back!" The Brunette said.

New Man strode toward the kitchen with a confidence that struck me as false, and I slunk after him.

In the kitchen, back to me, he popped open another bag of chips and carefully poured the contents out, spreading them around evenly on the platter. So wrapped up was he in arranging his chips just right, it wasn't until he pivoted to the fridge for the cheese that he found something blocking his path.

Me.

I glared up at New Man.

New Man nervously smiled down at me.

"Hey, buddy—"

I barked aggressively. But not so loud that the group in the living room could hear me, however. Think of it more as a series of low growls, but invested with all the menace and threat I had in me.

New Man took an inelegant little hop backward, eyes frantically looking toward the living room for assistance.

But if I could help it, there would be no help coming.

"It's OK," New Man said, both hands out in an *easy does it* gesture of placation.

As if I could ever be placated. As if.

"All I need to do is get past you," New Man said, "and get to the fridge, and get some more cheese for the nachos for—"

A part of me half admired him. He'd promised The Woman he'd make more nachos, and he'd deliver unto her more nachos, even if it meant negotiating his way around Hellboy, aka me.

Eh. Screw half admiration.

I barked even more vociferously, still keeping it quiet enough so the group couldn't possibly hear.

Then I saw a shift. New Man's nervousness appeared to subside, replaced by a slight annoyance.

"I need you to let me pass," New Man said. "This is unacceptable, maladaptive behavior."

Shift, schmift. I knew feigned bravery when I saw it, and this was as feigned as bravery comes.

No longer even attempting to contain myself, I let out a string of loud barks, drawing The Woman to us.

"Gatz?" she said, her voice filled with concern.

It occurred to me, then, that this was the first attention she'd shown to me all night. I might have been offended by this fact, but I was so relieved to have her kneel down beside me, rubbing behind my ears as I lapped happily at her face, I decided to shelve my pissed-off feeling for the time being.

"I, uh, accidentally stepped on his tail," New Man fibbed.

So, he was capable of telling a fib, huh? Fibbing may not be up there on the Ten Commandments, but maybe it should be. See, I knew this guy couldn't be as perfect as he seemed.

"Oh, is that all?" The Woman said.

All? ALL?

"I've done that too," The Woman said, waving a blithely forgiving hand. "Dogs and their tails, right?"

New Man smiled widely at this slightly odd thing to say, but that smile froze when he caught my glare, unseen by The Woman. His grin decreased yet further as The Woman nodded, bringing me back toward the living room with her.

New Man cleared his throat, and I turned back to catch him pulling open the fridge, which he could do now that I was no longer blocking it.

His eyes met mine, and I gazed steadily back, sphinxlike now, before turning tail.

In the living room, once the stepping-on-the-tail incident was related, an incident that hadn't actually happened, I received the soothing affections of the group, as was only my due.

I hoped that, from the kitchen, New Man could hear it all.

I hoped New Man realized who was really king of this castle.

Chapter Twenty-Three

Three weeks later . . .

The Woman brought me back much earlier than usual, but The Man was ready for us since she'd called ahead.

After the usual exchange of formal pleasantries, she was about to take her leave when he stopped her with a:

"STAY!"

He barked it so loud, no one could have blamed her if she assumed he was administering a command to me. Except he never yelled at me like that, no matter how bad I'd been. And his tone now wasn't admonitory so much as it was just plain loud.

"Stay?" she said.

"Or," he said, "go?"

"Do you want me to stay or go?" she said, understandably confused.

I was confused too. This was the moment I'd been hoping for, for so long; the moment when he'd do something to stop her from going out that door again. And yet now that he was doing it, I sensed he might be flubbing the whole thing.

"No," he said. "I mean, yes. Go. Go OUT!"

She sighed but not without a benevolent level of patient tolerance. "I think you're going to have to give me a little more to go on here."

"GATZ'S OFFICIAL BIRTHDAY!" was the little more that he came out with.

Her expression completely softened then as she said with a gentle wistfulness, "Gatz's Official Birthday."

And here's where I need to explain the one thing, outside of a regal bearing, that I share with Her Majesty, Queen Elizabeth II. QEII, as I like to think of her familiarly, was born on April 21, so that's her Real Birthday. But in England, her Official Birthday, the date the country celebrates it, is the second Saturday in June. I'm not really sure why, but if you asked me, I'd have to guess it has to do with the British weather. An April celebration would likely involve a high probability of precipitation. But have it in June, and at least you stand a chance at a good day.

In my case, no one really knows when my Real Birthday is. The obvious deduction is that it's sometime early in winter, but no one knows the exact date. So, after The Man adopted me and later The Man and The Woman became a couple, they put their heads together and decided that, like QEII, I would be given an Official Birthday. But unlike her, I wasn't given a specific Saturday in June. Rather, my Official Birthday was decreed as being "the first really amazingly gorgeous day that we're all home together."

And that Sunday, it was amazingly gorgeous out.

Now that The Man had shouted like a loon several times, he calmed down enough to explain, "I'd just been figuring that, when you said you were bringing him back early, it's so amazingly gorgeous a day today, this should be Gatz's Official Birthday this year. But then I thought that maybe you'd like to join us. You know, to make it extra special for him? But you probably have other plans, so—"

"I do," The Woman cut him off. "But I agree, it would be nice for us all to mark the occasion together. Let me just . . ." She pulled out her phone, punched some buttons, sent a text.

"So," she said brightly once she was finished texting, "where shall we go?" Not waiting for an answer, she added with a gleam in her eye, "As if I have to ask."

I gotta say, the walk to our favorite park was torture—torture in

terms of staying focused, that is. When you think about it, the pre-
ponderance of food trucks in the city is totally unfair to dogs. Who
doesn't want to stop at every purveyor of hot dogs, hoping for a little
questionable meat to hit the pavement? Who doesn't want to preen
for the falafel vendor, hoping he'll be charmed enough to toss over just
one spicy ball? The aromas were killing me! But . . .

*Gotta stay focused, Gatz. You're going to the park with your people,
the moment you've dreamed of but feared might never come again. Gotta
stay focused!*

What can I say? I did my best.

And being back at the park, our park, with the both of them—Both.
At. The. Same. Time.—it was every bit as good as I'd dreamed it
would be.

On that day, it was no mere repetitive game of stick. Oh no. There
was a stick. There was a ball. *And* there was a Frisbee.

They took turns throwing all three for me, and no one said, not
even once, "That's enough, Gatz. It's time to go."

They just played and played with me, even laughing together over
my antics. It made me remember how happy we'd been once, and I
hoped with all my might that it would remind them how happy we
could still be again.

I loved hearing them so generously say, "No, after you"; "Really, I
insist, after you," as each throwing implement was introduced. There
was such a feeling of love in the air, I wished it could go on forever.

But even I can't run forever, and eventually, I got tired out.

Still, no one told me it was time to go, but they did ask if I
wanted to.

"We could get ice cream," The Man suggested.

"It is your Official Birthday, Gatz," The Woman agreed.

I could not fault their logic.

Nor could I fault that they both held on to my leash, their fingers
touching as we walked for our ice cream, me between them. Just like
old times.

So, ice cream we had, but we had vanilla, as opposed to the chocolate we all knew could kill me. That was really great too. And seeing
The Man reach out to gently dab at some ice cream on her cheek, and
hearing her laughingly accept that dabbing—oh, the beauty of that
tinkling laugh—that was the best thing. These two just had to get
back together!

But the bittersweet thing about ice cream is that you can't keep
eating it forever. If you don't eat it with a reasonable level of speed, it
becomes a whole other experience entirely. And while I have a high
tolerance for messes, not everyone else feels the same.

"Time to go, Gatz?" The Woman said, popping the last of her cone
in her mouth and wiping her fingers on one of those crappy little inef-
fectual napkins they always give you.

She'd framed it as a question, but I knew that this time it was a
statement.

So she walked us back to our apartment, and as great of an Official Birthday as it had been, she still left afterward.

The Man went to his room to don a fresh flannel, since he'd drib-
bled ice cream on the other one. When he returned, the sun was
setting outside the window, and I wagged my tail at his feet.

"Gatz, no."

Aw, come on. Please?

I wagged my tail harder.

But it's my Official Birthday!

"I said no, Gatz."

*Do you think QEII has to beg to get her own way on her Official
Birthday? Or ever?*

"You know I hate to dance," The Man said.

I thrashed my tail against the floor, my tongue practically falling
out of my mouth.

The Man sighed.

I knew that sigh.

"Well, it is still your Official Birthday . . ."

YES!

"OK," The Man said, "but only for you, buddy."

I hurried to the other side of the room, waiting as patiently as I could, while The Man stripped down to his boxers and put on a pair of white gym socks.

Then, we slid across the hardwood floor toward each other à la Tom Cruise in *Risky Business*, and The Man sang "Old Time Rock and Roll" aloud, while I bounced along in time.

Yeah, I know. The dog being able to dance might be a suspension-of-disbelief bridge too far for some people. That's OK. Go look up "border collie line dancing" on YouTube. I'll wait here. Oh, and *that* border collie? He can play Jenga too! Hey, I'm working on it.

Here's something almost no one else but me knows: The Man's got a great voice. Dude can sing.

After that, I went to my toy basket and fished out the dance skirt, used solely for this purpose. The Man helped me get it on over my hips, and then he hoisted me up in the air over his head. I could almost hear the crowd cheering us on when I imagined them swooning as we reenacted "The Time of My Life" from *Dirty Dancing*.

Hey, no one puts Gatz in the corner.

Finally, The Man got fully dressed, took out two pairs of dark sunglasses—one for him and one for me—and we exited the apartment, hitting the sidewalk to "Stayin' Alive" from *Saturday Night Fever*, that imagined guitar lick strutting us into the night.

We may have had no time to talk as we passed the trees, fully in leaf now that spring had finally sprung, but that didn't stop the ladies from checking us out as we made our way to our watering hole.

Once inside, we had to take our sunglasses off, because otherwise we'd look stupid.

Flash forward to the next morning. We'd just seen The Lady From Last Night off, and while I was happy enough for The Man to have some companionship, so long as it remained meaningless—if only I could be as successful in telepathically sending the "Keep It Meaningless" mantra to The Woman; if she had a string of meaningless affairs like The Man was having, it'd have been fine with me—I was happiest to have him back to myself.

The Man headed for the couch, and I trotted along behind him, still feeling happy. It was therefore not until he sank into the couch and let out a heavy sigh that I noticed the change in his demeanor.

"I miss her," The Man said.

Of course, I knew he wasn't referring to the lady who'd just left. He was talking about The Woman.

I hopped up on the couch, slumping down beside him, instantly deflated.

Yeah. I miss her too.

Chapter Twenty-Four

Eight weeks later...

New Man and The Woman sat in the front seat of his convertible, driving out of the city and onto the highway, while I chilled out in the back seat, a travel scarf blowing over one shoulder, feeling the bliss of the wind in my fur from the top being down.

Where were we going? you may well ask.

The Hamptons.

We were going to the Hamptons.

And I was OK with this, because it was, as The Woman had explained to me, a working weekend.

Me, I'd assumed we were done with New Man. I hadn't seen him since he'd come to Book Club so many weeks ago; and good riddance, said I. But I'd heard her talking on the phone with her folks, saying she didn't think she could make it this year, something about needing to do some work with one of her authors, and while I knew she wasn't his editor anymore, maybe it was like The Redhead had suggested—that, sometimes, they'd still want to discuss craft stuff? After all, The Blonde may have been on the same level as The Woman, but we all knew she wasn't as incisive of an editor, so maybe New Man just wanted her informal input? Anyway, from what I gathered, her family said she should just bring the author in question along, so there we were.

And I was especially OK with this because I just love the beach.

I may be a city dog at heart—plus, that's where The Man is—but there's just something about the feel of wet sand squishing between my paws, and the sunsets over the water are spectacular. In the city, sunset is simply the orange ball disappearing behind a building. But at the beach? So many colors! And if you take the time to watch the whole show, it's just so dramatic.

What can I say? I have an artist's soul.

Specifically, we were going to The Woman's family mansion, which came into view once we'd traversed a long, narrow, and bumpy dirt road. New Man may've been worried about what it might do to his transmission. Me, I was just enjoying the amusement-park feel of it all.

As we pulled up to the huge lawn of the sprawling white estate, some of The Woman's family spilled out of the front door, while others came at us from around the sides of the building, circling the vehicle before we'd even fully stopped.

Her mother, her father. Her two brothers—who I think of as Tall and Short—and their wives and children. Whether in bathing suits, khakis, or Bermuda shorts, they looked like one giant Gap ad, all excited for the Fourth of July weekend ahead, but even more excited for . . .

"GATZ!" the family greeted me collectively.

It being a convertible, it was easy for me to hop over the door and greet them just as eagerly in return, accepting their adoration with licks as they gathered around me. There's nothing like a reunion of family. At moments like these, happy as I was, I felt sorry for The Man. When it came to family, the poor guy didn't know what he was missing. And that's not just a figure of speech. Having been brought up in the family he had, he just really didn't know.

While me and the fam were playing Old Home Week, I suppose New Man and The Woman unloaded the car, because now they appeared before us, New Man carrying all the bags except for The Woman's beach carryall.

"Welcome, welcome!" The Woman's Father said.

"It is so lovely of you to join us for the holiday weekend!" The Woman's Mother said, clasping her hands together.

"It was so lovely of you to allow me to stay at your home," New Man said, flashing a grateful smile.

I saw it immediately: instantly, they were all charmed by him.

But I couldn't hate, not in the moment. I was too busy accepting all the love as the little kids squealed, "Gatz!" anew each time it was one of their turns to pet me.

New Man gestured to the bags in his hands. "If someone could show me where to take these . . . ?"

Tall volunteered, leading him away.

They were barely out of earshot, when The Woman's Mother turned to her.

"He's so much friendlier than the last one," she said appreciatively, squinching up her shoulders as she let out a girlish giggle.

"'The last one' wasn't just some passing thing, Mother. We were together for three years."

You go, girl. You tell her, girlfriend.

"Still," The Woman's Mother said.

"It's a working weekend," The Woman said. "Nothing more."

The Woman headed for the house as her mother turned her attention to me, waiting happily at her feet.

"What do you think, Gatz? I know I can always trust you for the real poop."

I think it's like The Woman just said: "Nothing more." And with me around, that's the way it's going to stay.

Chapter Twenty-Five

Same day . . .

Yes, I was living the life of Riley here.

Lounging on a stylish beach chair beside the gorgeous infinity pool, the surrounding area covered by The Woman's even more gorgeous, model-beautiful family members who were frolicking in and around the pool and on the lawn—The Woman had promised we'd hit the beach later—I had my Wayfarers on to protect my eyes from the damaging UVA rays.

Peace. I was totally at peace.

At the end of the beach chair beside mine, The Woman and New Man were giggling over something. The Woman looked as stunning as you'd imagine in her bikini, which managed to be both tasteful and incredibly alluring. But New Man? It was practically obscene how good he looked in his swim trunks.

The Woman held a bottle of sunscreen out to New Man.

"Would you mind?" she said. "I can't reach."

"No problem at all," he said.

No problem at all, I might've mimicked, in a mocking singsong voice, but the weather was too nice for pettiness. I got out of the city so rarely. I just wanted to enjoy my brief break from all the hustle-bustle madness while it lasted.

And so it was that I watched, unconcerned, as New Man slowly massaged sunscreen onto The Woman's back, gently easing his fingers beneath her straps and all along the edges of the top and bottom of her suit in order to ensure that not a single square inch of her insanely soft skin got burned.

When you think it about it, it was very thoughtful and considerate of him, being that thorough about it. And while some others, looking at them there, wouldn't describe what they were seeing as "a working weekend," I knew *exactly* what I was seeing.

You see, growing up with a writer like I did, I'm privy to a lot of insider info that the average layman or laydog might not have. For example, something I've heard a lot in my day is that even when a writer isn't writing, they're *always* writing. *Life* is writing. *Life* is learning and creating and building material. Like the late, great William Goldman said in *The Color of Light*, the greatest novel about the writing life ever written, "It's all material."

And, I supposed as I sat there, the same must be true about editing as well. New Man and The Woman might not look to the untrained eye like they were editing, but the Gatzer knew: they were hard at work, dedicated to their livelihoods.

Not long afterward, New Man and The Woman were swimming in the pool, splashing each other and generally cavorting. I was too busy sunbathing to pay them much mind, but then I caught sight of Tall. His wife was trying to tell him something, but his eyes, narrowing slightly, were glued to New Man and The Woman.

I knew what he was thinking, because I was thinking it too.

It looked like New Man and The Woman were still busy editing. They should really give that work thing a rest.

Enjoy yourselves, kids! It's a holiday!

Chapter Twenty-Six

That evening...

Everyone was gathered around an incredibly long table set up in the yard. The table looked rustic, but I'd bet anything it cost a mint. Overhead, colored lanterns hung, and tiki torches lined the perimeter. The Woman's Mother and The Woman's Father were at either end of the table, with everyone else lining the sides. I was a few feet away munching on the burger The Woman's Mother had set out for me on a Lenox plate.

This, however, was not just any burger. It was the very best filet mignon, the meat ground up so fine it practically melted the instant it touched my tongue.

I tell you, these people really knew how to throw a barbecue.

There was plenty of good-natured sibling banter going on between The Woman and her brothers, and she'd just finished telling them all about the new novel New Man had written. As it turned out, they all knew who he was. They were all fans.

Yeah, I thought, *you just keep writing those megaselling* New York Times *bestsellers, pal. The Man is a real writer. He's literary.*

What can I say? If it's in service of The Man, I'm willing to put on my snob hat.

"It's exactly what the market is looking for right now," The Woman said. "It's refreshing. It's different. Everyone at the publishing company feels really good about it."

The Woman and New Man shared a look, which I caught, as did Tall. The look on Tall's face was similar to the one he'd had when we'd all been poolside earlier in the day and then some. It was slightly skeptical but somehow without malice and very brotherly.

Short was too caught up in his burger to notice anything. In my experience, Short is all about the food.

"This is delicious," New Man said. "Did you make all this food?" he asked her parents.

"It would've taken them days," The Woman said.

"Not to mention," Short added, "if our parents had cooked, everything would be charred."

The Woman's parents laughed good-naturedly, and New Man laughed more heartily than the mildly amusing line warranted. Still, he was clearly enjoying all of their company as much as they were enjoying his. It was practically a mutual admiration society, with the possible exception of Tall.

New Man went to take a bite of his burger, but then his eyes met mine and he stopped. It occurred to me then that I must have been glaring at him from the sidelines. Despite my determination to have a carefree weekend, it was hard to completely let my guard down. There was too much at stake.

It should've given me satisfaction to see how unsettled I made him, so much so that he lowered his burger to his plate, bite untaken. And yet it didn't. I didn't want to be this petty dog. I wanted to be Gatz, Friend to All Beings.

Turning my attention back to the delicious food still on my plate, I resolved to do better, be better.

At least for the weekend.

"How come you're not home for the weekend?" Tall asked New Man. "Why aren't you with your own family?"

"My family lives in the Midwest," New Man said. "A bit hard to pop over for the weekend. I do make it home for the major holidays, though, and family events, and of course I have them here too."

"But not this weekend, huh?" Tall said. "That must be some heavy-duty work you two were doing today, to keep you away from your family."

"Um, yes," New Man said. "There were just some things about the book that we still, uh, needed to discuss."

"Riiiiiight," Tall said. "But why live in New York at all? It must be hard to be so far from your family."

Was it just me, or did Tall not completely trust New Man?

"I know my sister has authors all over the country," Tall went on.

"It is hard," New Man said, "sometimes. And I know I could write in any state, but . . . I don't know. Something about the city always felt right to me. I could never quite put my finger on it."

I looked at The Woman. I could've sworn there were stars in her eyes, but I was sure it was just the reflection of the hanging lanterns. Although when I looked around at the others, no one else's eyes looked like that, except for New Man's.

"That's cool," Tall said, "I guess. So, you married?"

The Woman almost never does anything that's not one hundred percent elegant, but how else to describe red wine flying out of a person's mouth? Her eyes shifted to Tall, digging into him.

"*Hey,*" she said threateningly.

"What?" Tall said, all defensive innocence.

"Not cool," Short said, mid-burger bite, mouth already full of food. And for once, I sensed he wasn't commenting on his food.

"What?" Tall said. "What's wrong with asking if the guy is married? Mom and Dad are married. You and I are married—"

"Not to each other, thank the Universe," Short cut in.

"And most people this guy's age"—Tall ignored Short's weird interjection, pointing a fork with purple potato salad on the end of it at New Man—"are married. So I don't see anything wrong with asking—"

"He's an author with a book coming out from my publishing company," The Woman said. "It's unprofessional to ask that."

"Hey, you brought him to our *family's* Fourth of July Weekend bash. What am I supposed to do, refrain from discussing everything but business?" Not waiting a beat, he turned once more to New Man. "So, are you married?"

My burger bites slowed, and I watched New Man stiffen in his chair.

"No," he said, "I'm not."

"Ever been?" Tall pressed.

"Come on—" Short started.

"Still not asking strange questions here," Tall insisted.

"No," New Man said, "I haven't."

"And why is that?"

"*Dude!*" from The Woman.

"What!" Tall barked back at her.

"You gotta admit," Short said, "that's pretty invasive."

And I gotta admit that if I was looking for someone chill and fun to hang with while knocking back some great filet, it'd be Short by a country mile. But if I ever needed someone to defend my honor in a bar fight, it'd be Tall all the way.

"Do you really want to be *that guy*?" The Woman asked Tall.

"I'm not being *any guy*. All I'm doing is asking a simple question—"

"A simple invasive question," Short corrected.

"It's not an invasive question. Hey, Gatz!"

I put my head up, alert.

"Do you think it's an invasive question?" Tall asked me.

I love when they loop me in.

"I think it's an invasive question," Short said.

"Is your name Gatz?" Tall asked.

"I only wish it was. It's such a cool—"

"I hadn't found the right person before," New Man said, slicing straight through the banter.

Thanks a lot, pal. I was just about to give my answer.

But no one was looking at me anymore. The group had all turned to New Man.

"Say that again?" Tall said.

"I'm not married," New Man stated steadily, "nor have I ever been, because I never found the right person before. I don't know, I . . . I believe in that."

He looked so vulnerable then and somehow sweet too. Certainly, everyone at the table looked touched by his words, and even I had to lower my eyes in acknowledgment of the sweetness of it all. It sounded like New Man believed not in settling for good enough. Rather, he believed in True Love.

As did I.

"That's really sweet," Tall said, playing foreman of the jury.

New Man nodded, clearly embarrassed.

"Never mind all that . . . *emotional stuff*," Short said, leaning forward. "What I want to know is: Tell me about the perks! An author who does as well as you do, there have to be some mighty fine perks."

Leave it to Short to forsake the heart of the matter to get at the heart of the matter.

New Man looked a bit uncomfortable at this line of questioning—perhaps he was one of those people who don't like talking money, politics, or religion with people he just met? Not that I could blame him. Still, it did make me wonder: Just how rich was this guy? I mean, The Man was well respected for his work. We lived OK. Could New Man really be living that much better? Somehow, I doubted it. They were both writers, after all; they both put on their pants one leg at a time, so how much difference could there be? And yet, people seemed to always be asking him about it.

"Um, I do OK," New Man said.

See? I thought. *The guy does OK—same as us!*

"But what about the perks?" Short pressed. "Like . . . a wine cave!

Have you ever been to a wine cave? Do you have one? I've always wanted to go to one of those."

I had no idea what a wine cave was, but given The Woman's family's own state of wealth, I saw no reason why Short couldn't just go to one if it mattered so much to him.

"Um, no wine caves," New Man said. "Sorry."

"Look," The Woman said, "it's not all unicorns and rainbows. There are downsides."

"Name one," Tall put in.

"Well," The Woman said, "he does have a stalker."

Well, that got everyone's attention.

I'd first heard New Man's stalker mentioned briefly back at Book Club all those weeks ago, but then The Blonde spilled her wine and the world got sidetracked, kind of like when you're trotting down the sidewalk, thinking you'll head one way, but then a car zooms by in the other direction and you think: *I'll just go that way now!* Attention is *hard*.

But now I got the whole story. Apparently, New Man's stalker— "hardly a perk," he took pains to point out—had been his fan since the release of his debut novel, the one book that didn't sell very well until the books that followed all became bestsellers.

"I'm sure she's harmless," New Man said. "Or, at least, I hope she is."

"You answer your fan mail," Tall said, sounding surprised.

I was still stuck on him *getting* fan mail. Did The Man get fan mail? I knew he got tons of emails from other authors, asking for one kind of favor or another, but I didn't think he really got fan mail.

"Of course, these days," New Man said, "it's too much."

Too *much* fan mail?

"I have to have my secretary read them," New Man went on. "Then he replies to most of them and just flags the ones for me that he thinks I'd want to see or the ones that require a more personal reply."

And now I was stuck on something else: a secretary. Dude had a secretary? We didn't have one of those!

"So you're saying everyone gets some kind of reply?" Tall said.

"Well, yes," New Man said. "Years ago, when I was still trying to break into the business, I read an interview with a bestselling author in which she said she didn't answer any of her fan mail; that she always intended to, but it just seemed too onerous a task. That really bothered me. I thought: 'You get to live your dream—you get to make your living as an author—and you can't be bothered to thank the people who gave you that life?' I can't tell you how much that bothered me. I further thought, 'Hey, no one likes writing thank-you notes, so if it's too much for you, hire someone to do it! You can afford that!' Anyway, I vowed to myself then, if I ever became as lucky as she was . . ."

He let it trail off.

"So, everyone gets a reply," Tall said.

"Everyone gets a reply," New Man said, "even if now I have to pay someone else to write most of the replies because if I did it all myself, there'd be no time left for writing books. But in the beginning, I did do it all myself, and the stalker is a holdover from those early days."

"She's very proprietary," The Woman said. "She sends him these emails all the time. She tells him the things she likes, but she gets particularly offended when she finds things in his books that she doesn't like. It's almost like she feels a sense of ownership over him and his work. She got *very* upset when he changed the author photo on his website."

"I don't want to make too much of it, though," New Man said. "It's not exactly *Misery*-level stalking, and, I don't know, I guess I just feel sorry for the poor woman."

"That's . . . generous of you," Tall said.

New Man nodded, clearly embarrassed again. Uncomfortable with the attention fixated upon him, he stood, lifting his plate.

"Can I get anyone else a burger while I'm up?" he offered.

I perked up at this, woofing and wagging my tail at the offer. So what if the offer was coming from New Man? Paraphrasing Shakespeare: a great burger is a great burger. For wisdom, you can't beat the Bard.

Chapter Twenty-Seven

Same evening...

After dinner and dessert—strawberry shortcake and chocolate cream pie, the latter of which I was not allowed to partake of—The Woman invited me for a walk.

"How about some quality time, Gatz?" she offered.

I was kind of surprised she'd leave New Man to Tall's devices, but I figured she trusted Short to intervene, should it become necessary.

Thus, we found ourselves far from the madding crowd, perched at the end of the dock, her dangling her toes and me my tail in the cooling water.

Tired after all the lounging and eating I'd done that day, I slumped over a bit, half asleep in her lap as she craned her neck around to watch the group from afar. New Man had hit it off with all the nieces and nephews, running around trying to catch fireflies and playing games with them like hide-and-seek and SPUD.

The Woman smiled softly to herself, rubbing the backs of my ears as we heard the sound of rustling footsteps approaching in the grass from the other direction.

It was Tall.

"Hey," Tall said.

"Hey," The Woman said.

"Walk?" Tall offered.

At the word "walk," I was all ears, thoughts of tiredness behind me as I leaped to my feet.

The Woman laughed as she hopped up to join me.

Soon, we were walking, farther away from the group on the lawn. I heard loud laughter coming from the group, and I turned to see that someone had brought a Frisbee out. There's not much in life more tempting than a Frisbee flying, sailing through the air invitingly, and I longed to run over and join them. But an even bigger part of me wanted to know what The Woman and Tall would talk about, and I tuned back in just in time to hear her say, laughing:

"That's not what I said!"

"It is!" Tall said. "I was fifteen!"

"Uh-huh."

"And we were fighting with my bedroom door."

"Uh-huh."

"You were trying to keep me in, and I was trying to get out."

"I recall."

"And when my fingers got caught in the doorframe and my pointer finger was cut off—"

"It was only the tip! They sewed it back on!"

"*And when my pointer finger was cut off*, you said to me, 'Good, I hope it hurts and you're bleeding.'"

Whoa, I had no idea The Woman had such a vicious streak in her.

"I did not say that!" she objected.

Phew! I didn't think she would, not really.

"Oh, you definitely said that," Tall said, but not like he was mad or anything.

"OK," The Woman relented, "maybe I said that. But do you even remember what we were fighting about?"

"No."

Something told me he was lying.

"*Really?*"

"OK, fine, I probably deserved it."

See? I would've bet anything she'd have had just cause, and I would've been right.

The two erupted in laughter.

We were still leagues away from the others, the faint sounds of joy and merrymaking catching my ears even from the distance. The Woman must've caught it too, because I saw her eyes travel toward the sounds, eventually latching onto New Man, who seemed to be happily in the center of all the little kids. If my eyes didn't deceive me, they were making a maypole out of him and he was letting them. I had to admit, it looked like fun—the idea of holding a ribbon in my teeth and then running around him until he was wrapped up like a mummy—but I believe in dancing with the one who brought you, and in this case, that was The Woman.

But if I saw The Woman locking eyes on New Man, Tall took note of it too.

"No way this is a working weekend," Tall said. "You like this guy."

This was the second time I'd heard someone say something like this to The Woman. The first time, it was The Redhead during Book Club, when she cornered her in the kitchen. And now Tall was saying the same thing, here.

Anxiety hit me like a truck.

No, no, no, no—

"Come on, no," The Woman said.

Phew.

"Don't do that," Tall said.

"Do what?"

"That! I know you. You like this guy."

"I don't."

"You do!"

I could tell she wanted to hold her own, and I wanted her to hold it too, but it was like her eyes were magnetized, and I panicked as she shifted her gaze once again to *him*.

"You're looking at him right now!" Tall said, stating the obvious, which was necessary since she didn't seem to get it. Part of getting over a problem is first admitting you have one.

"So?" Tall insisted. "Is there something between you two?"

It was an endless beat of her, nervous and harried, looking at him and him looking at her with a wide-eyed expectancy, and it got real gloomy for me in the gloaming there as I waited in agony to hear what she would say.

Finally, she opened her mouth and—

"Gatz! Gatz! Gatz!"

The nieces and nephews bounded in our direction, demanding that I show them attention, demanding that I allow them to shower me with love.

It was one thing to remain firm when they were far away. But I was powerless to resist the call to play now that they were all so close.

And so I allowed myself to be dragged away from the conversation until I could hear Tall and The Woman no more.

Chapter Twenty-Eight

Same night . . .

On our way in for the night, we'd passed a few random family members out on the back porch, whispering over their wine. Short, notably, had been juggling the remains of the strawberry shortcake and chocolate cream pie on his knees, alternating bites of each.

Who was this "we"? you may ask.

The "we" was New Man, The Woman, and me, heading inside to hit the hay.

I trotted beside them down a hall with many closed doors, all of us falling somewhere on the continuum of tired after the full day we'd had. Two of us looked like we'd had a totally lovely evening (them), while one of us was more on the fence about things (me).

"I loved it," New Man was saying as I tuned in. "I hope they did too."

"Are you kidding me? Those kids somehow manage to get so bored here by the end of the first day, they were thrilled to have you with them."

It seemed to me she was exaggerating his role. Sure, they'd loved maypoling him. I mean, I would've enjoyed mummifying the guy too. But who was it they screamed "Gatz! Gatz! Gatz!" for whenever they caught sight of him?

Picture me lowering my eyes as I humbly rest my case.

Reaching a door at the end of the hall, they at last stopped, and I sat back on my haunches between them, like a nun with a ruler at a middle school dance.

"Well," The Woman said, "this is me."

"Nice door."

"Thank you."

"Is that oak?"

"Mahogany."

"Mm."

"And you are . . . ?"

New Man gave a chin nod toward the opposite end of the hall. "Your . . . *overly inquisitive* brother put me *all* the way down there."

"Right. Of course he did."

"Yes. Of course."

The two emitted almost identical happy sighs, smiling over me as they looked at each other. I might as well not have even been there.

New Man started to step forward, so I leaned into The Woman with my furry forehead, using my snout to nudge her farther back toward the door to her room.

The two blushed awkwardly, but whatever. At least he wasn't moving toward her anymore.

"Well, good night, then," The Woman said.

"Good night, then," New Man echoed back.

Eventually, they managed to tear their gaze from each other, New Man heading off to take that long walk down the hall, while The Woman turned the knob on her door. I watched her watch him go, but he didn't see her watching, since his back was turned. Then, as she pushed the door open, I saw him look back over his shoulder at her. But just like he hadn't seen her looking, she didn't see him looking either. So no one saw anything.

Except me.

I saw it all.

Thankfully, the door was soon safely shut behind us, separating us from all the dangers that threatened from beyond. If I could've done so without drawing attention to myself, I would've leaped up and down until I secured the lock.

OK, so maybe that would have been going too far.

The Woman performed her nighttime ritual in the en suite bathroom, while I curled up at the bottom of her massive childhood bed, awaiting her return.

She soon rejoined me and, with a loving "Good night, Gatz," accompanied by some final presleep petting, fell fast asleep, dreaming whatever she dreamed about.

Me, I was still wide awake, chewing on my tail.

For the first time since we'd driven out of the city, it occurred to me to guiltily wonder: What was The Man doing? In my mind, I pictured . . .

The Man's apartment, living room, nighttime. Trying to write and struggling. Eating an entire pizza by himself while watching The X-Files. *Trying to write some more, struggling some more. Pacing around with his thoughts, knocking back a few Buds. More X-Files. More struggling non-writing. Cleaning out an already clean fridge, sadly empty with the exception of a few more Buds, a jar of mayonnaise, and a few turkey scraps.*

Certainly, he wouldn't attempt to go out; he wouldn't even try anything social without me.

Cracking open one of those remaining Buds, lying on the couch, crying over a black-and-white romance movie.

Yup, that sounded about right.

I curled further down in the bed, wistfully looking at the empty space next to The Woman. Gosh, how I wished The Man were right there, filling that space. And I knew that, whatever he was doing back home, he wished for that too.

My chin slumped onto my paws, my snout disappearing beneath the sheets.

Chapter Twenty-Nine

The next day...

The next day passed in much the same fashion as the one that had gone before: more enjoying the perfect weather, more lounging by the pool and walking down to the beach, more quality time spent with family, more amazing food, more me being adored.

More of New Man and The Woman editing.

So imagine my surprise when, latish in the afternoon as I was doing laps in the pool, New Man and The Woman disappeared briefly into the house, only to return with . . .

"What are you doing with your suitcases!" The Woman's Mother cried. "We're doing the fireworks tonight!"

I suppose I should comment, albeit belatedly at this juncture, on how odd it was that The Woman's *British* family celebrated the Fourth with such fervor or even celebrated it at all, given what the holiday was supposed to commemorate. But I guess when some people move to a different country, they just go all in.

"We want to beat the traffic," The Woman said.

Wait. What? We were supposed to have another night and day here. Sure, if I stayed too long, I'd start to miss the variety of takeout delivery places the Naked City had to offer. But I was willing to make the sacrifice of eating filet mignon burgers for another twenty-four hours.

But, apparently, it wasn't up to me.

What fresh hell was this Universe I was now living in, where Gatz's opinion wasn't solicited at every turn?

I leaped out of the pool, shaking my water-soaked fur all over New Man so he'd know exactly how I felt about this change of plans.

"But it's only Sunday!" her mother objected.

Exactly.

"Right," The Woman said, "and if we wait until tomorrow, the roads will be a madhouse."

Gee, for an editor, she wasn't making a lick of linguistic sense. How could the roads (outdoors) be a madhouse (indoors)? I mean, am I wrong here?

"Work early Tuesday morning," The Woman went on. "You know how it is."

No, I really did not. And I don't think anyone else did either, except maybe New Man, who stood beside her in tacit agreement to her plan of action.

Oh well.

There was nothing for it, nothing to be done as there were rounds of kisses and hugs all around, New Man shaking hands or politely bestowing cheek kisses where appropriate as he thanked everyone profusely for their graciousness in opening their lovely home to him.

Then I was hopping into the back seat, suitcases beside me. And while I'd been unsettled by our early departure, I soon forgot all about that, no longer questioning the abrupt change of plans, once I realized that this meant time for me to ride in an open vehicle, bumping down the suburban road and then zooming along the highway, the wind dancing through my fur.

At one point, I was sacked out in the back with my tail over my eyes, listening to The Woman and New Man speak in hushed voices up front.

"I couldn't wait to get out of there," The Woman said.

"I know," New Man said.

Why? I loved that place!

Sometimes, I have to marvel at the idiocy of humans. Little kids who quickly grow bored of wide-open spaces and room to play, and these two adults right here . . .

Oh, an infinity pool. Oh, meals I don't have to make myself that just happen to be otherworldly delicious. I can't wait to get out of this hellhole!

Please. Spare me.

"It's so hard keeping the secret," The Woman said.

Immediately, alarm bells started pinging around my brain.

Secret? What secret?

"But we agreed, it's only until the book comes out, right?" New Man said.

"Right," The Woman said. "Here's to that accelerated pub date. The end of the year can't come soon enough."

What secret???

I caught New Man nervously eyeing me in the rearview mirror, and I bared my teeth in a silent growl. Even though he was seated behind the wheel, driving, I could've sworn his body managed to take a little jump of fright backward.

Still . . .

"My place this time?" New Man questioned, with what sounded something like bravery in his voice.

"Your place this time," The Woman firmly affirmed.

WHAT SECRET???

Chapter Thirty

That evening . . .

New Man's building was gorgeous on the outside, taller than all the other buildings in the area, so I had to crane my neck all the way back to take in the full height of it.

Inside, it was even more impressive.

And the elevator? Don't get me started.

I grumpily lay on the elevator floor by her feet, grumpy because I was feeling out of sorts, out of sorts because I felt like I was out of the loop . . . on something.

New Man put a special key into the panel, into a slot beside the letters PH.

Ooh, he had a special key. Ooh, he was a fancy guy.

How. Annoying.

I stared at the numbers as we rose, and rose, until . . .

"Here we are," New Man announced with a determined brightness as the elevator doors opened directly onto his massive foyer and the living room beyond.

I'd seen such places in movies before, but I'd never seen an apartment like this in person. The Woman's family was wealthy, practically beyond a dog's wildest dreams, but even their glamorous apartment in the city wasn't like this.

Whatever bad mood I'd been in earlier was forgotten as I took in the vast indoor space.

It.

Was.

Beautiful.

Before me was the living room with its gorgeous modern couches. Vaulted ceilings. Art Deco detailing on the walls. Lighting fixtures that were like architectural feats of magic cascaded down from the high ceiling. On the wall opposite, massive drapes concealed a window that, if the size of the drapes were any indication, spanned the entire massive wall.

I'd never seen anything like this.

If you asked me, *no one* had ever seen anything like it.

OK, obviously New Man had seen it before. And the person who designed it. And the Realtor who'd sold it to him. But you get my drift.

I stood frozen there in my Elizabeth Bennet moment, like I was seeing Pemberley for the first time.

And as gorgeous and expensive looking and well chosen as everything was, I had to admit, it wasn't sterile. Rather, there was a sense in the air of home, a sense of love.

Photos of family members. Personalized mementos. *Nope, not sterile.*

I was entranced.

From somewhere else, I vaguely heard The Woman ask, "Do you want anything?"

What more could I possibly need? I thought.

But then, still only vaguely registering other people talking, I realized she must've been asking New Man when he replied, "Whatever you're having."

I came to enough to register New Man easing past me, bags in his hands, and I trotted in the direction The Woman's voice had called from.

I found her in the kitchen, grabbing wineglasses directly from a particular cabinet, taking a wine opener from a specific drawer.

She seemed so confident about it all, none of that awkward trial-and-error stuff New Man had engaged in as he'd negotiated his way around our far tinier kitchen that time he'd been there for Book Club.

Well, of course she was confident. Of course she wasn't awkward at all.

She was The Woman.

She was pure grace.

And she was still pure grace as she poured wine into the two glasses as New Man entered the room, doing that awkward clap thing humans do sometimes when they're hoping to get something going.

"So," New Man said. "Gatz."

I was ready for my Robert De Niro moment.

You talkin' to me?

"Would you like a tour of the place?" New Man nervously offered.

Wait. There was even more to see of this place?

I started to eagerly wag my tail but then caught myself. No way was I going to give in to his charm offensive.

Swiftly, I tucked my tongue back into my mouth, transforming my eagerness into a more appropriately gruff-and-tuff attitude, like:

I mean, I guess that could be OK . . .

But then, as I trotted along behind him, I let my tongue hang out as often as warranted, so long as he couldn't see me back there.

"This is the dining room," New Man said, with a *ta-da!* gesture. "It's really only for fancy occasions."

Some people in the city had entire separate rooms for eating? The Woman's whole entire clan could've fit comfortably around that long table. And the hanging Tiffany lamps were to die for.

"You're welcome to eat here, of course," New Man added, "anytime."

I felt required to scoff.

This place was like something out of a Disney movie. Like: lame. Like: Where's *your* singing candelabra?

But as we exited the room, I passed one on the sideboard.

Huh.

From there, it was off to the master bedroom, where my jaw almost literally hit the floor.

You could get lost in that bed! I'd lose so many toys in that thing, oh my gosh . . .

"Sorry it's a bit of a mess in here right now," he said.

What was he talking about? The place was spotless.

Anyway . . .

I reeled in my awe. I mean, I guessed that spaciousness would be appealing to *some*. But who needed lost toys? Gosh. Some people could be so inconsiderate.

"And I have a new tennis ball for you!" New Man announced.

Wait. Was this guy trying to . . . *impress* me? *But who cares what he's trying to do?* I thought, my head darting upward, unable to resist.

Lo and behold, New Man had produced a fresh tennis ball, which he was holding in his hand.

Could there be anything more appealing than a brand-spanking-new Spalding? Its fluorescent yellow-green surface so pristine, just waiting for me to chase it around, the first to defile it?

Sweet mother of god . . .

New Man threw it across the room, and I wanted to run after it. Oh, how I wanted to run after it. But I had to restrain myself. Honestly, it physically hurt to do so.

Don't give in, don't give in, don't—

"All righty then," New Man said with confused resilience when I failed to retrieve the ball of perfect temptation. "Maybe later? Onward."

Onward was to his en suite bathroom. My life was feeling very en suite all of a sudden.

Oh. Oh wow.

You'd think a person or a dog might get tired of viewing stunning room after stunning room, but I hadn't been there that long, and it hadn't happened yet. Who knew what might be possible in this crazy world of ours? Maybe in my next life, I'd be the new Le Corbusier. Plus, there were so many great smells that I ached to explore.

The counter was gold-plated while the floor was a mirror, for crying out loud. I became fascinated with that floor, pushing my snout up against the surface, one-eyeing my own handsome reflection.

"Isn't that cool?" New Man said, appreciating my appreciation. "I think this room is a little flashy, but this is the way it was styled when I bought it."

Maybe, if I hadn't been so caught up in admiring myself in the reflective surface, I would've taken note of the fact that, throughout the penthouse, one of the smells that I was smelling was that of The Woman, even though she hadn't accompanied us into these rooms. And if I hadn't been so caught up in admiring myself, I would've taken more serious note of some of the other things I was seeing in that room, things that would come back to haunt me later—a second toothbrush on the counter, a makeup bag on the ledge behind the toilet, a familiar shade of lipstick—but I didn't. Well, if everyone looked like me, they'd be doing what I was doing too.

But even I can only take a thing so far.

Realizing that maybe I was making too much of a . . . *display* of myself, I pulled back, appalled at my own behavior. Then I squinted at the floor.

Wow, streaky much? This place was awful, just awful. Disgusting!

I was relieved to get out of there with my sanity intact, trailing behind New Man out of the bathroom and down the hall in a veritable daze. I figured I'd seen it all.

"There's a doggy bed set up over here for you too." New Man indicated. "And a fully stocked toy basket over here."

Not that the words meant any more to me than the sounds they made at that point, verbal symbols without concrete association.

"Oh, and one more thing," New Man said.

I could feel my eyebrows contort at this. How much more wonder could one dog take?

If I were to give New Man credit for anything, it'd have to be that the guy sure did know how to build to something, and everything had all been building up to this.

New Man reached up and pulled a cord near the front draperies or pushed a button or both or who knows. Who knows what magical act of prestidigitation he committed then? All I know is, the draperies came apart, separating and traveling silently and slowly along their tracks until the entire wall-sized window was revealed, my eyes going wider by the second.

And there it was:

The entire city.

Lit-up buildings as far as the eye could see. It was stunning; it was whatever the word is for something that is beyond absolutely stunning.

It was the most beautiful nonhuman sight I'd ever seen in my life.

And it was all at my feet.

I was speechless.

But just because I was speechless, it didn't mean that everyone else was. Vaguely, I became aware of voices in the kitchen.

"Here," The Woman said, offering something. Perhaps one of the glasses of wine I'd seen her pour before?

"Thank you," New Man said.

But they were just words, background noise.

Slowly, I made my way closer to the glass pane, staring out in awe. Involuntarily, I raised a paw, placing it gently against the glass.

Romantic music began playing in the background. Something slow. Frank Sinatra. Well, what better choice? It was his city too, after all.

I sensed movement, followed by shapes reflecting on the glass, but I was oblivious to it all, unable to wrench my gaze away from the view. The rest of the world had fallen away from me.

Who knew that something so simple could be so beautiful?

If I'd paid more attention to those reflections in the glass, I'd wonder later, what would I have seen? A man and a woman, foreheads resting against each other? Tender kisses? Two people very comfortable with each other, physically? Two people dancing?

But I didn't see. I wasn't paying attention.

Instead, I dropped to the floor, letting my chin rest there, relaxing into the view until it was as though I was one with it. My entire being was total bliss.

And what might I have seen if I'd paid attention then?

The dancers no longer dancing. Holding hands, walking away from the frame made by the window. Leaving the music to play on, until eventually the click of a door closing filled the space.

I may not have seen, but I did hear, that decisive *click* finally breaking my trance.

Quickly, I turned around to see . . . no people.

I rose, then, trailing after that click, curious to find where The Woman has disappeared to. New Man? Not so much.

Down the hallway leading toward the master bedroom with its impossibly spacious bed, the one where toys could easily get lost, I paused briefly to survey the photos on the walls.

New Man as a kid with a younger girl, probably a sister. New Man with the same sister, all grown up. It seemed like they'd always been close, never the type to smash each other's fingers in a door and then gloat about it. Not that there's anything wrong with that. New Man and his mom, all the love in the world toward each other.

I almost smiled at that.

Sometimes, I missed my mom, even though I couldn't really remember her anymore. I wondered where she was now, if she was even still alive. And if she was still alive, I wondered what she'd make of me and my life now.

But then a noise came from the master bedroom, and the nearly formed smile died on my face.

Curious, I trotted closer, stopping short of attempting to push into the room when I got there.

The sounds coming from the room were similar to the ones I'd heard the first time The Man brought The Woman home and they'd shaken the mattress together, but these sounds, they weren't awkward. They were comfortable. They were loving.

My mind raced, a multitude of emotions overtaking me: shock, pain, panic, betrayal.

I know what they're doing in there! And I've heard what first times sound like, this is NOT what a first time sounds like!

I gasped as the full realization of the enormity of it all sank in:

THESE PEOPLE HAVE DONE THIS BEFORE!

Chapter Thirty-One

The next day...

Many hours later, too many to count, the sun rose on a new day to find me still positioned just outside the master bedroom door, sitting sentry. I was awake but exhausted. Were I to go and check out my reflection in the mirrored floor of the bathroom, I'd no doubt see fur bags under my eyes. I hadn't slept at all last night.

So close was I to that door, The Woman practically tripped over me when she opened it to emerge. Her legs were bare, and over the top portion of her body she had on an oversize pale-blue button-down shirt, not what she'd had on the day before. It was not a garment I'd ever seen on her in my life.

It smelled of *him*.

"Gatz!" she cried. "What are you doing here, buddy?"

She leaned down to scratch me behind my ears. The scratching helped a bit, but I just felt so glum.

"You haven't been out here all night, have you?"

Obviously.

"What is it? What's wrong?"

I heard the sound of footsteps and looked up to see New Man standing over us.

I glared at him.

He stared back at me.

"Do you know what's the matter?" The Woman asked him.

New Man shook his head, clearly preoccupied.

"I have to grab something," he said. "I'll be right back. Don't move."

Well, of course we were going to move. What did he think we were going to do, play Statues here for his amusement?

New Man disappeared back into the bedroom.

"Let's get you some food, buddy," The Woman said. "You must be starving."

In the hours I'd spent sitting sentry, I'd ignored all bodily functions, so great had been my worry. And over the course of that dark night of my soul, there were times I thought I might never feel hunger again. But at the mention of food, my stomach growled and it occurred to me with a shrug: Huh. I could eat.

I jumped up and trailed after her, excited at the prospect of food.

Trotting into the kitchen, I saw her lean down to a bottom cabinet from which she removed two bowls—quite similar to my bowls at her apartment and at The Man's place—and a can of food: it was my favorite brand. Before she closed the cabinet completely, I glimpsed stacks of cans of that very same food.

Huh, again.

I hadn't seen evidence of any other dog here.

Certainly, I hadn't smelled one.

Oh well, I figured, *whoever he or she may be and wherever he or she may be, that dog sure has good taste.*

But as she went to the sink to fill the bowl with water, the puzzle pieces began fitting together in my head, and the solution they added up to did not fill me with happiness.

You'll think me an idiot for not figuring it out sooner, but you try spending a sleepless night during which your fool head is filled with all manner of free-floating anxiety, and see how logical you are.

All those toys New Man had shown me yesterday, the new doggy bed, and all those cans of food . . .

Were they always planning on bringing me here? But they never, they didn't even ask me if any of this was OK, they didn't ask me if I wanted . . .

The Woman placed the two bowls in front of me, water and food.

"Here you go, buddy," she said.

A short time ago, my stomach may have been grumbling, but now I couldn't think of consuming anything. I couldn't think of accepting any form of sustenance.

My world was falling apart.

Instinct took over then. I took my snout and, with all the force I had in me, overturned both bowls, sending water streaming and kibble pouring across the previously pristine floor.

"Gatz!" The Woman cried, appalled at my behavior in a way I'd never heard her be before. "What is the matter with you today?"

YOU'RE what's the matter with me today! I barked. *How could you even THINK about being with someone else in a way that's not meaningless?!*

With a weary sigh, which was something else I wasn't used to The Woman directing at me, she got out paper towels and other supplies and began cleaning up the mess I'd made. She was on all fours doing that, facing away from the doorway, when a voice behind us asked:

"Is everything OK?"

New. Man.

When I'd seen him briefly earlier, I hadn't noticed what he was wearing. I'd been too busy glaring at him. But now I saw he was bare chested, the bottom half of his body covered with loose light-blue pants that appeared to match the top The Woman wore. *Pajamas.* They were sharing the two halves of a pair of pajamas. How much worse could this get?

Everything was *not* OK! How could she not see that he wasn't The Man?

"Yes," she said. "Gatz just knocked over his food."

The Woman was still too busy chasing after stray bits of food to notice New Man's nervousness, but I did. He swallowed, hard, and then a light mist of sweat broke out over his upper lip.

I stared up at him, wondering what he was up to.

New Man cleared his throat, swallowed again.

"I hope this doesn't seem too sudden," New Man started.

He nervously glanced down at me, but I certainly wasn't about to offer him any support. Whatever this was, he was on his own.

"It's just that," New Man went on, "I don't want to wait until the book comes out at the end of the year. It feels right *not* to wait, and . . ."

New Man's hand disappeared into a fold in his pants, and that's when I realized for the first time that the garment had pockets.

New Man started to pull a small box out of his pocket, and I zeroed in on that half-emerged box, panic rising as he said, while The Woman looked up from her project on the floor:

"I hope you both will agree to—" New Man started.

NOOOOOOOOOOOOOOOOOOOOOOOOOOO!

I lunged at New Man, knocking the box across the room before she could see it, nearly knocking New Man over too in the process. He may have outweighed me by about eight to one, but I was mighty in my panicked fury.

But if I was mighty, New Man was instantly enraged.

"Gatz, what are you—" The Woman started to say, only to be cut off by New Man shouting.

"YOU STUPID DOG!"

Silence.

The Woman and I stared at New Man, wide-eyed and in shock. To his credit, New Man looked shocked too. Ashamed, even. For a long moment, we all just froze like that.

"What was that?" The Woman demanded to know.

"I don't know," New Man said, crestfallen. However he'd envisioned his day going, it hadn't been like this.

You and me both, pal.

"But I thought you liked dogs," The Woman said, a hesitation entering her voice.

"I don't *dis*like dogs." New Man hesitated, squirmed, delayed. "But I avoid them whenever I can."

The Woman stared at him in disbelief, and I stared at her.

"*What?*" she said, sounding a little angry and a little betrayed, but also very, very sad.

New Man gestured at the tiny scar beneath his eye.

"When I was little," he said, "I was attacked by one."

"You told me that was from a fall at the park," The Woman said, eyes narrowing.

"I lied," he said simply.

The Woman swallowed, digesting his admission.

"I want to be OK with them, but," New Man said, a boyish wistfulness in his eyes, "I never really got over it." He paused. "It was an English mastiff."

Seriously? That was pretty much the largest breed out there!

I pictured a tiny junior version of New Man, like the photos from his childhood lining his hallway. I pictured that little kid squaring off against an English mastiff.

In the moment, I couldn't fault him for being scared. I'd have been scared too!

"But Gatz isn't an English mastiff," The Woman objected, somewhat exasperated. "Look at him: he's so little!"

"What can I say?" New Man shrugged, not indifferently, but rather, philosophically. "It's a fear. No one said fears have to be rational. They're fears."

The two stared at each other, wordless, knowing what they now knew.

As for me, my brow furrowed as I disappeared into my head, wondering:

How did I miss all this? How did I miss them growing a relationship so big that he'd bought her a ring and was going to ask her to marry him? When did it—

Realization dawned then, as a series of imaginings came at me, filling in the blanks.

On a Sunday night, she'd have dropped me off at The Man's. On Monday, she'd have gone in to work only to find New Man waiting outside her office. A smile blazed across her face.

Nighttime, a weeknight, her place, maybe a week later: More laughter, more pages, rising contentment and joy. That night he came to her place for the first time. Lots of working, but also living. And laughing. So much laughter.

Lots of Chinese takeout containers around too, the definition of human fun.

She brings me home on a Friday, spends the weekend with me. But after that one time he came on his own and the other time he came to Book Club, he never comes on the weekends again. But as soon as I'm gone . . .

Somewhere in there, the tension grows too great, the tension of being unable to be together, and she hands him off to The Blonde, so The Blonde can become his editor, so The Woman is ethically in the clear and then they can . . .

As soon as I go back to The Man's on Sundays, New Man returns. Maybe they open a bottle of wine, talk over books and writing, someone lets their hand linger on the bottle too long. They both stare at the bottle.

They both stare at each other.

"Why do you think I always say I'm busy on weekends?" New Man said, drawing my attention back into the room.

I could almost see the hearts broken on the floor.

"I knew if I came to your place again," New Man continued, "he would terrorize me."

"Terrorize you?" she said, skeptical.

"Yes. Whenever you're not in the room, whenever you're not looking, he's always growling at me and . . . doing hostile things."

"Gatz isn't hostile!"

"He has been. To me."

The guy wasn't wrong about this, but I certainly wasn't about to validate him.

"But if you don't like being around dogs," The Woman said, "if you don't like being around Gatz, how can this work? How can *we* ever work?"

The words hung in the air.

Chapter Thirty-Two

A little later...

We left the way we'd come, on the grand elevator, only this time we were going in the other direction, taking the long way down.

And this time, there was just the two of us.

Back at the apartment, with nothing left to say, The Woman had quickly gathered up her things. New Man had tried to plead with her, like it was the most important thing in the world to him, and in that moment, I truly and one hundred percent respected him for the first time: the idea that he'd fight hard for what mattered. But when he could finally see there was no point and that he was only making her sadder, he let her go. He didn't want to make her sadder; he didn't want her to be sad at all, and I could respect that too.

Now we stood side by side on that elevator. She was back in her own clothes, a toothbrush sticking out of her bag.

She looked more worn down by life than I'd ever seen her, her clothes wrinkled, her eyes red.

Me, I couldn't help but be relieved. What a narrow escape!

Having completed our elevator ride, once we reached the revolving front doors, I bounded outside into the bright, shiny day, excited, waiting for her to join me on the sidewalk.

I turned to her, my tongue hanging out, and all the elation went out of me.

There was a teardrop on her lower lash, threatening to fall. And then it did fall as she crumpled down the side of the building.

I'm not saying she was a wreck. The Woman is *never* a wreck. But she did look defeated.

I put my front paws in her lap, licking the tears from her face, and she smiled at me.

"Thank you, Gatz," she said.

She placed her beautiful hands on the sides of my face and stared into my eyes.

"You're always there for me," she said. "I love you."

She kissed my forehead and stood, shaking it off.

"Let's go get breakfast," she said.

A little pep back in my step, I trotted happily beside her.

It was all going to be OK. She'd get over it. He was never The One.

Chapter Thirty-Three

One week later . . .

The Man was hunched over the laptop that sat on the round table by the window, tapping away furiously.

Me, I was chewing on my tail, staring off into space, deep in thought, contemplating the mysteries of the Universe.

OK, so maybe only the chewing-on-my-tail part is true.

The Man gave out a happy sigh.

Wait.

The Man's sighs were never happy!

The Man leaned back in his chair, staring at the screen, a look of euphoria washing over his face.

Wait. Happy? And euphoric?

"The end," The Man said, sounding stunned. Then: "*THE END!*"

My brows furrowed. Geez, I hoped The Man wasn't going to turn into one of those guys you see on street corners screaming about Armageddon at passersby. Sometimes, I'm a passerby, and that always wigs me out.

"Gatz!" The Man exulted, raising his arms in *YES!* mode, "I finished my book!"

I dropped my tail, shocked.

Book? He wrote a whole book? How did I miss that?!

Just as I'd done the previous week at New Man's apartment, envisioning what must've transpired between New Man and The Woman over the past few months whenever I wasn't around, I now envisioned what The Man must've been up to; again, whenever I wasn't around.

The Woman drops me off and leaves. The Man flops down onto the couch to watch TV.

Days and nights pass. The cycle repeats. I'm dropped off by The Woman, The Man hangs out with me during the week, The Woman comes back to pick me up.

Eventually, one time when I'm gone, The Man ventures over to the laptop.

As the days and nights pass, whenever I'm gone, he watches less and less TV in the middle of the day. He dresses a little better, real pants instead of sweatpants, like he'll be more upbeat about the writing if he's more upbeat about his appearance. He eats less and less pizza for breakfast—a sound body is a sound mind.

Slowly but surely, his days and nights become committed to writing on his computer—the work has always been so important to him—and he looks almost . . . happy.

Before long . . .

My mouth was agape as I turned my attention back to the room.

Well, goddamn.

While I wasn't looking, The Man wrote a whole book.

And now The Man was on the phone, about to burst with the excitement of it all.

"Come over!" he told whoever was on the other end. "I've got something to show you!"

I'm not sure how long we waited after that. An hour? Two? All the while, The Man tapped nervously on his knees. I felt lucky he didn't play knick-knack on his knee, although it'd have been nice if he'd given the dog a bone while we waited.

Knuckles must've barely grazed our door and The Man was jumping out of his seat and bounding toward the door, throwing it open.

It was The Editor.

Normally, I'd be unhappy to see him there, since we did not get on, but The Man was so excited to have him over, so I figured: What the heck? I could be gracious.

"Hi," The Editor said. "You—"

But before The Editor could utter another word, The Man was herding him into the apartment, with barely a "Hi" back, and straight over to the computer.

"What?" The Editor said. "I don't even get offered a lousy beer this time?"

"Not today," The Man said, placing his hands on The Editor's shoulders and forcing him down into the chair The Man usually occupied behind the laptop.

The Editor seemed about to object, and I couldn't really blame him—no one likes to be manhandled, unless you're into that kind of stuff—but then something on the screen caught his attention, and all was silence from that quarter.

The Editor read.

The Man paced.

The Editor read some more, The Man paced some more, leaving nervous energy all over the room.

For hours, it went on like that, The Man breaking off his pacing upon occasion just long enough to look over The Editor's shoulders, see where he was at.

Through it all, I watched them both.

You might not think it fascinating to watch someone watching someone else reading, but I was totally gripped. Watching the eyes of The Editor dart back and forth, it reminded me of my favorite TV sport, tennis, and I found my eyes darting back and forth too. I just love the *thwack, thwack, thwack* of a good tennis match, and I just *know* in my heart that Rafael Nadal *must* love dogs.

Hours later, the light had disappeared from the sky. Previously, The Editor's eyes had gone back and forth quickly, moving like a really zippy old-fashioned electric typewriter, like he couldn't wait to get to the next part. But now his tracking eyes had slowed considerably, like he was savoring, like he didn't want what he was doing to ever end.

By now, I was nearly asleep on the couch, eyes at half-mast but still observing. The Man was hunched over the couch, knee tapping, staring into space.

I think we both sensed the energy in the room shift at the same time.

The Editor stared at the screen for a long moment, eyes unmoving, and then slowly he closed the laptop.

At the click, we both jumped to our feet and paws, respectively, looking at The Editor. We were expectant. We were damned nervous.

The Editor took a breath.

A part of me wished he'd hold it forever, and not out of any lingering animosity toward him. What if I was wrong? I'd been wrong a lot lately about things. It used to happen so rarely, like almost never, but lately I'd been on a bad streak. What if I'd been reading his body language all wrong? What if he wound up being as disappointed in this book as he'd been in the one The Man wrote after The Woman moved out? The Man had handled that crushing disappointment once—could anything worse happen to The Man than literary disappointment? Losing The Woman, sure, or losing me. But outside of those two things, nothing affected him more, and I doubted he'd survive such a blow a second time.

"It's—" The Editor started to say, only to have The Man cut in with an eager:

"Get you a beer?"

"Now you're offering me a beer?"

"Or water," The Man said, more eager still. "Or, hey, how about an entirely different beverage? A beverage that's neither beer nor water? Whatever you want. I could even go out, hit the local bodega, and—"

I knew what The Man was doing. He was delaying what he'd begun to worry might be the inevitable. The Editor must've known it too, because he held up a hand to stanch the flow of what would undoubtedly be a litany of every beverage known to man and, once The Man finally closed his mouth, intoned the simple words:

"It's good."

Ah, mercy.

I felt the sweet relief wash over me, and I know The Man felt it too. Who is to say who felt it more keenly? Of course, it was his book, so you'd think he'd feel it more deeply. But when you love someone, really love them, their pain is your pain. And so, their relief at avoiding pain becomes your relief too.

"There's a lot of pain here," The Editor said.

Pain: it seemed to be one of the themes of the day.

"But it's not at all surfacy," The Editor qualified, using what I was sure was not a technical term; I was sure Max Perkins never used *surfacy*. "Unlike with your previous effort, this doesn't come off at all self-indulgent. It's got a lot of heart, and everything in it feels so real, so true."

A weight had clearly been lifted off The Man's shoulders. The Editor hadn't finished, however, because then he added the incredibly healing words:

"This is the best thing you've ever written."

The Man released a breath, the exhale carrying away with it so much that had been wrong since she left him.

"I guess I'm still a writer after all," The Man said with a confidence I hadn't seen in, maybe ever.

"You've always been a writer," The Editor said, going on to speak words that won me over once and for all. "The best writer I know."

Chapter Thirty-Four

Minutes later...

There was the sound of the front door closing, footsteps walking away.

After delivering his verdict, The Editor didn't tarry, not even staying an extra minute when The Man offered again to get him a beer.

"Just because you're brilliant," The Editor had said, "it doesn't mean I'm going to start drinking Budweiser with you."

In what felt like a past life, I'd have been offended by this, on The Man's behalf. But The Editor had made The Man so happy—happy!—and I couldn't fault him for a thing. Everything was jake with us now.

The Editor gone, The Man collapsed onto the couch, staring up at the ceiling, mesmerized by the wonder that is the world.

As quickly as he collapsed, though, that much more quickly did he leap to his feet.

"Let's celebrate, Gatz!"

After all this time, we had our routine down pat, so soon we were down the street in the doorway to our favorite watering hole, prepared to make our grand entrance. The Man had on a fresh ball cap, and I'd done my best to groom myself with my tongue. If you ask me, that's the one thing cats have over us dogs: they self-groom perfectly. I guess it's because they're just so bendy. Me, I need regular baths to get at the hard-to-reach spots I sometimes miss.

The bartender pushed our drinks across the bar at us before we'd even sat down, which we did, swiveling to scope out the room.

"Oops!" The Man said. "In all the excitement, I forgot to do something."

I tilted my head, questioning.

"I have to see a man about a dog."

I tilted my head harder.

"I, uh," The Man said, embarrassed, "I have to take a pee."

Ahhhh, euphemisms.

Spare me your literary devices, human, and call a pee a pee. Everyone does it and we all gotta go sometime. We're only humans. And dogs.

"Come on," he said, insisting I come with.

You'd think he'd be willing to trust me on my own for a few minutes, but I knew where he was coming from. It wasn't me he didn't trust; it was all the other people. Who knew what sort of nefarious person might try to take me home with them if they saw me sitting there all by my handsome lonesome?

I leaped down off my stool.

Not much more than a minute later, we were side by side in front of the urinal, him standing, me wagging my tail encouragingly at his feet; The Man can sometimes get uncomfortable with public urination. So while The Man was doing his business, I was simply offering moral support.

The bathroom was pretty seedy, with real characters moving in and out around us. There was also a heck of a lot of graffiti everywhere. On the back wall behind the urinal, in classic black Sharpie, someone had written: *For a good time, call Hannah.* Whoever wrote it had even helpfully provided a phone number.

The Man zipped up his pants, turning to me with a wide grin.

"Whatddya think, Gatz? We like a good time and we're supposed to be celebrating." He waggled his eyebrows. "Should I call Hannah?"

I tried to get into it. Really, I did.

I thumped my tail, I let my tongue hang, I even attempted a leer.

In short, I did all the elbow-elbow/nudge-nudge things one would expect from a good wingdog. But here's the thing: it was all feigned. My heart just wasn't in it.

Whatever enthusiasm I'd had for meaningless affairs was gone.

A memory came to me then, a memory of a scene I'd imagined just a week ago.

New Man and The Woman open a bottle of wine, talk over books and writing, someone lets their hand linger on the bottle too long. They both stare at the bottle. They both stare at each other.

OK, so maybe it involved a lot of just staring, and maybe the bottle thing was kind of weird, but that had more romance in it than this.

Even if The Man was obviously kidding about calling Hannah.

As had happened so many times before, because we are that close, The Man must've read my mind. OK, maybe not all the finer details, but he definitely got the gist.

He let out a sigh, *not* a happy one.

"I think I've been deluding myself," The Man said.

I looked down at my paws, back up at The Man. For his part, he looked over the writing on the wall, and from the way his eyes were going, I'd bet anything his mind was moving quickly.

"I need something more than this."

And, just like that, I was in panic mode.

Oh no! Not you too!

Chapter Thirty-Five

That same night...

We arrived home, both in our own heads, each occupied with our own thoughts.

The Man moved toward the window, taking in his own view of the city. It was much smaller than New Man's, but it still had beauty.

Me, I headed straight for the bathroom. Once inside, I shook my booty at the door, slamming it behind me. I then proceeded to pace up and down the tiny bathroom, still panicked.

Why was I so panicked? you may well ask. Well, it went something like this:

What am I gonna do, what am I gonna do, WHAT am I gonna do? First, The Woman meets someone new, and I think I'm doing a fine enough job of keeping them apart, come to find out they've been TO-GETHER PRACTICALLY THIS WHOLE TIME WITHOUT MY KNOWLEDGE! Then, I FINALLY get her to see that he's not The Man, I FINALLY get her away from him, and The Man hits me with this. He needs something more than meaningless? MORE than MEAN-INGLESS? How much longer can I realistically keep them from other people? He is not allowed to find a New Woman. They both want more, so how can I keep them from—

I froze in my tracks.

Wait... He's single... SHE'S single...

I bounded toward the living room, intending to exit the bathroom but completely forgetting the door stood between me and it because I'd slammed it. I therefore crashed into the door, which was not ideal, causing myself to tumble over backward. Thankfully, the power of my energetic bound had popped the door open from its flimsy old-fashioned frame and I was able to leave with no further ado.

Not taking the time to pause to perform a concussion protocol, I leaped into the living room.

The Man was still deep into his contemplative state, which I easily disrupted with my loud entrance. He looked up to see me crashing across the room toward him.

"What's up, buddy?" he asked.

I jumped over the couch, soaring across the remaining feet that separated us and crash-landing into the wall next to the stereo.

Still not bothering to run a concussion protocol.

The Man came over to see what I was up to, but I ignored him for the moment, all my attention focused on manipulating the stereo buttons.

I'm not going to lie and say I got it right the first time. That would be too hard to believe.

So maybe it took me a few shuffles, but through trial and error, I eventually found exactly the song I was looking for: "When I Was Your Man" by Bruno Mars.

When in doubt, I always reach for Bruno Mars. Bruno is my jam.

As the opening bars blasted out, I bored my eyes into The Man, begging him to get the message.

I gazed with wistful longing toward the bedroom, hoping he got the point about the same bed feeling bigger without the one you love to share it with you.

"Gatz, what do you—"

I turned toward the stereo, shaking my head sorrowfully at the sheer pain of it all. What must it be like to hear your song—*your song*, the one that you chose together—playing once she's gone?

"Buddy, I don't understand what—"

The pain of hearing friends talking about the person you broke up with, after the fact.

OK, so maybe they didn't have any friends in common, never had, but not every line can correspond in a one-to-one relationship with an individual's pain and heartbreak. Even Bruno Mars isn't enough of a magician to pull that off. Still, I made the most of it, going with it as best I could. I nodded knowingly; I gazed heartbroken at the heavens.

"Is there something going on in your life that I should know about?" The Man asked.

Your life, you idiot! Doesn't your heart break a little every time you hear The Woman's name?

I looked straight at The Man, back to full wistful.

And now we were at the part of the song where Bruno is almost howling.

"Gatz—"

Taking my cue, I jumped into the famous prelude to the chorus, throwing back my head and letting loose with an accompanying anguished howl of *"OOH-OOH-OOHOOH-OOOOOOOH!"*

"OK," The Man said. "Sure."

You're not all that young, and you really should have brought her flowers, dude!

I became less theatrical in my, um, theatrics. Instead, I let my eyes do the talking, dog to man.

After a beat, so long it made me begin to doubt his intelligence, I saw the light dawn in his eyes as the chorus played through.

Because you're an idiot, she had to go dancing with someone else!

"But that's just it, Gatz. She's with another man." He sighed. "It's over."

As the music continued, I vehemently shook my head no. If I was going to succeed in getting one thing through that thick beautiful skull of his, it had to be that, no, she was no longer with New Man. They were kaput. Finito.

"What do you mean, no?"

Thank you, Jesus.

"Gatz, she's with that famous author, that guy who's always on the stupid *Times* bestseller list. I know because—"

I shook my head again. Between me and Bruno, we were doing our best here. Could he not get a clue?

"I know because the craziest thing happened. An email came through on the contact form of my website."

Seriously? We were going to talk about his fan mail at a time like this? But I thought we already established that he doesn't really get any. It was probably just another author, asking for a blurb. Or spam, in which case: just delete!

"The email said that the two of them were a couple. The writer, who didn't sign it, seemed to expect me to do something about it. But what was I supposed to do? We weren't together anymore. But when I tried to reply, to inform the anonymous writer of that fact, it bounced back as undeliverable. I told myself it was just some crazy prank, because I wanted to believe she hadn't moved on, but then I saw the two of them together in a coffee shop one day when I went out to get the papers while you were still sleeping and, well, I could just tell." He paused. "Remember that commercial fiction bestseller's book she gave me on our first Hanukkah together?"

For once, he didn't wait for my response.

"It's *that guy*. And, damn! His author pic? That guy's so handsome! Why'd he have to be so handsome?"

I shook my head again, so hard this time, I thought it might fly right off my body.

"She . . . She's not with him anymore?"

More headshaking, but a little less vigorous this time. It was time I exercised some caution. The old noggin was taking a heck of a beating.

Thankfully, my level of vigor proved sufficient. I could see that The Man was processing what I was telling him, beginning to doubt what he thought he knew.

"But that . . . But that doesn't mean she'd want to be with me again . . ."

Bruno was getting ready to wail again, and I was right there with him.

"OOH-OOH-OOHOOH-OOOOOOOH!" I joined in again.

"I don't know what that means," The Man said.

Stop being so dumb! You're not that young!

I moved in front of the stereo, jabbing my snout at him repeatedly to indicate the words were about The Man.

Flowers, hand-holding—you need to put in the work if you want to have a relationship, dude!

I looked into The Man, and I could see he was really getting it now: more flowers, more hand-holding, less being a douche. OK, I added that last one, but come on, you know it's true. And anyway, it's *implied.*

But now that The Man was finally getting it, his defenses were wearing down and he just looked so sad and lonely.

Well, I guess it can't be easy, realizing you've been acting like a douche.

You should've spent more time focusing on her. When you had the chance, that's what you should've been doing.

The Man had started shrinking into himself. As depressed as he'd been since last Hanukkah and Christmas, this was worse, seeing that he'd missed his best shot at that brassiest of brass rings: True Love.

You should've taken her to every party she ever wanted to go to. All she wanted to do was dance!

The Man's head went up as he finally grasped the true wisdom of Bruno Mars.

Aha!

The Light Bulb Moment.

"Dancing . . ." The Man mused.

Suddenly, it was like his whole face was suffused with energy, and I started leaping up and down, nodding vehemently all the while.

"I could take her *dancing*," The Man said.

I looked up at him with all the joy and love in the world.

Yes.

Chapter Thirty-Six

Same night; so late, it's practically a new day . . .

The Man gulped as he hit #1 on speed dial on his cell phone and placed it to his ear.

See? Even after all these months, even though they'd broken up, she was still #1 on his speed dial. She'd always be his #1.

He looked to me for support, and if I could've, I would've given him a thumbs-up right then. Instead, I settled for jumping up and down until he got the message, turning on speakerphone.

Hey, I'd architected this whole thing. The least he could do was let me hear both sides and not have to rely on his secondhand report of the She Said part of things later. Secondhand reports can be so unreliable. You almost never get all the nuance.

I tried to picture what things would look like in her apartment. I pictured her being ecstatic at being finally rid of New Man, but then I remembered the pain in her voice after they'd split up, and I knew that was just wishful thinking on my part. What was more likely? The Woman would be lounging across her bed reading a book, in cozy yet chic clothes. She'd be looking fairly downcast, having trouble concentrating on the text.

Yeah, that sounded about right.

Then her cell phone would start to ring, and she'd pick it up, concern washing over her face when she saw the number on caller ID. Sure enough . . .

"Is everything OK?" were the first words out of her mouth.

Not exactly the reaction The Man had been expecting, made evident when he responded with, "Um, hi to you too?"

"You only phone, instead of texting, when something's wrong with Gatz. What happened? Is Gatz in trouble? Did he eat something? Is he lost?"

"Oh no! Gatz . . . Gatz is fine!"

I pictured her shoulders relaxing at that news, relieved if not a little annoyed that he hadn't opened with that.

"Oh, OK," she said. "Well, good."

"He's fine, maybe a little depressed and anxious lately, but largely he's OK."

"Oh, um, OK."

"Yeah, I think he's OK."

"That's great." Long, expectant pause, but when no more was forthcoming: "So, why did you call tonight?"

The Man froze. Still not able to master the thumbs-up thing, I nodded at him for moral support.

"We should get together," The Man said abruptly.

"What?"

"Yeah, I thought we could . . ."

I looked at him encouragingly, but The Man, frozen in fear, could only shrug back, like: Eh. He got nothing.

"You thought we could what?" The Woman prompted.

I gestured with my snout toward the stereo, hard—one, two, three times. *Come on, dude, just get it already. Don't make me put on Bruno Mars again!*

And . . . epiphany.

"DANCING!" The Man practically shouted. Way too loud and way too awkward, but we'd just have to find a way to work with it.

I pictured The Woman pulling the phone away from her ear, wincing at the volume.

"What?" she said.

"YES! DANCING!" Clearly, he was still having trouble with the volume. Thankfully, he modulated it as he continued with an enthusiastic, "You and me. We should go dancing! . . . Dinner and dancing!"

I really wished I could see her face for real right then. Was she charmed? Amused? Had she missed his frantic awkward energy and was now recalling it with a fond smile?

"You never wanted to take me dancing before," she said.

"Well, I do now."

This time, even though I couldn't see it, I could hear the smile spread across her face.

"OK, yes," she said simply. "Why not? That would be great."

"Great! Yeah!"

Me, I was beating my tail against the hardwood floor, ecstatic.

"When did you want this dancing to occur?" she asked.

"Um . . . tonight! How's tonight? No time like the present."

"To-tonight?"

"Sure! Why not?"

"Well, it is almost midnight . . ."

"Midnight, schmidnight! This is the City That Never Sleeps! The Big Apple! We can sleep when we're dead! Buried six feet under!"

"No time like the present"? And "the City That Never Sleeps"? For a literary writer of his stature, respected in highbrow circles throughout the world even if his royalty checks never reflected that high level of respect, he sure was trotting out all the old clichés tonight. The next thing you know, he'd be telling her, "the night is still young" and "you only live once." Well, just so long as he didn't abbreviate it to YOLO. Because then I'd know the guy had really gone off the deep end.

Still, I couldn't really fault the guy. It must be bizarre to have believed you'd lost the love of your life forever only to see that maybe, *maybe*, you had a second chance. So no one should fault the guy for failing to break out the Flaubert.

But if The Woman didn't fault him for that, she did have an objection to raise.

"I have to be up for work in six hours," she said.

"Right, right, work, uhh . . ."

"How about Friday?" she suggested.

"Friday. Friday? Friday! Friday would be perfect!"

"OK," she said, laughing softly. "I'll see you Friday."

Who cared if what he'd said had been riddled with clichés? And that he'd said "Friday" too much? It was working!

"I'll see you Friday," he said.

She hung up the phone then. I'd bet anything she was smiling shyly to herself.

The Man disconnected his end too, and then we just looked at each other for the longest time, wonder in our eyes.

We could barely contain ourselves.

Chapter Thirty-Seven

Four days later ...

The Man was frantically preparing for his date.

Wait. Dare I call it a date?

Sure, why the hell not!

He really was putting an effort into his sartorial preparations. No flannel shirt over a T for this momentous occasion; he'd actually broken out a classic oxford button-down. He even put in some hair gel. I did, however, have to nudge him toward the khakis. Let's face it, The Man is hopeless without me.

Finally, I grabbed one of his fancy leather dress shoes in my teeth, dragging it over to him.

"Gatz, I don't have time for Throw the Shoe right now, buddy!"

I did my eye roll thing, dropping the shoe at his feet, staring at him until he got it.

"Oh, riiiight. Real shoes, not sneakers."

That's right. We're adulting now.

As he dropped to the side of the bed to put the leather shoe on, I rushed off to try to find the other one in the chaos that is the bottom of his closet. Shoe partner located and delivered, I headed for the living room, figuring that before departing—*ON. THE. BIGGEST. NIGHT. OF. HIS. LIFE.*—maybe he might need some alone time.

Thus I was boredly looking over the *New York Times* when he finally emerged a short time later. He did a little twirl to show off for me. He'd traded up from my suggested khakis and was wearing a suit. A *suit*. The Man had put on a gosh-darned suit. Well, blow me down.

"So?" he asked, soliciting my opinion. "What do you think?"

What did I think? I let my tongue hang, panting my contentment. I thought he cleaned up pret-ty darned good.

"Do you think the flowers are too much?" he asked, anxious.

He was referring to an enormous bouquet of red roses, which he'd come home with earlier in the day and were now lying on the coffee table. The Man had gone out. The Man, rather than simply calling a florist and having them deliver the flowers to our door, had actually left our apartment and walked to the florist, so that he could select the flowers in person. He was totally Bruno Mars–ing the shit out of all of this.

I adamantly closed my mouth to hide my tongue contentment in answer to his question: No. The flowers were not too much. Nothing could ever be too much if it was for The Woman.

"OK," The Man said. "Wow."

Wow, indeed.

It was like he was trying to psych himself up because he was insanely nervous, but also like he was delaying a bit. I totally got that. Yes, he couldn't wait to see her, to once again be in her presence in a potentially romantic capacity, but he was also scared that he'd somehow screw it all up and then that would be that. Like if it never started, he could never spoil it, in which case the possibility of it yet happening would still exist somehow and somewhere in the Universe.

Yeah, I got all of that. He had a lot on the line here. Well, you and me both, pal. You and me both.

"You do think I look OK?" He sought verification.

I barked my fool head off in affirmation.

"Dinner . . . dancing . . . wow. OK."

He looked himself over in the wall mirror, checking his hair repeatedly. Then he moved to grab one of his ball caps from the coat-rack.

I admit it: I growled.

"Right, right," he said. "Leave the hat."

I thumped my tail, showing my approval. Hey, I can play Carrot and Stick as well as anyone.

The Man checked his capless hair one more time. I knew he felt naked without his caps, but for once he was just going to have to deal.

"OK. OK. OK! OK."

He looked to me, took a deep breath, and smiled.

"OK, buddy, I'm gonna head out now. I'll tell you everything when I get home."

I hope not! I hope you come home with her!

"I'll see you soon."

With one last breath in and out, The Man charged out the door.

Phew! He'd been procrastinating so much, for a moment there I worried he was going to make himself late. Relieved, I relaxed onto the floor, at peace. So much peace. But then . . .

The flowers. *He left the flowers.*

Oh no. Oh no no no no—

I grabbed the flowers in my teeth, bounding toward the door, heedless to the occasional prick of thorns. As I think has been previously established and documented, I'll do almost anything in the service of love.

True Love, that is.

At the door, I started to bark, loudly, praying for The Man to hear me, praying for The Man to come back.

But The Man didn't come back.

Come back! Come back! You forgot the flowers!

After a while, I had to concede that it was hopeless, and so I gave up, dropping the flowers dejectedly.

God, sometimes I wish he could hear me when I'm talking. I'm not asking for him to be able to hear me all the time, because that would be weird. But if he could just hear me during the occasional super critical moment, it sure would be nice.

I sighed, sulking, until . . .

It was then I experienced my own Light Bulb Moment.

Hmm . . . flowers . . .

Chapter Thirty-Eight

Same night . . .

Just like I only knew about what happened with The Woman and
New Man that first time they met in London was from paying attention when she told her work girlfriends about it, I only know what
happened with The Man and The Woman—first at her apartment,
then at the restaurant, then at the dance club—because The Man
told me all about it afterward. And it all went something like this . . .

The Man knocked at her door, like you do.

He felt like he waited forever for her to answer, but it had probably
only been a minute. He figured she'd used that minute to steady her
own nerves, hand on the doorknob, and then she opened it. But
would she really have been nervous? Or was The Man simply project-
ing his own psychological state onto her? It's always so hard to be
certain when you don't witness a thing for yourself.

Even though he'd last seen her just five days ago, when she'd
dropped me off on Sunday night, she looked to him like she'd grown
even more beautiful.

"Hi!" he said.

"You look," she said, taking in his own appearance from gelled hair
to fancy leather shoes, "incredible."

"It's really good to see you."

"You too."

And it was.

The words may have seemed mundane, on the surface, but it all just carried so much . . . *meaning*.

They stood in the doorway for a long minute, just grinning at each other.

"Are you . . . ready to go?" she finally prompted.

Suddenly, he remembered what he'd forgotten.

"Flowers!" If he hadn't realized that he'd have looked like an idiot doing so and stopped in time, he would've hit himself on the side of the head. "Shoot, shoot, shoot . . ."

"You were going to buy me flowers?"

"I did buy you flowers."

"And you left them at home."

Sheepishly, he nodded.

"Well," she said sincerely, "it's the thought that counts."

He was a great author, given to the occasional cliché. She was a great editor, given to the occasional cliché. See what I'm talking about? Made for each other.

"Is everything good?" she asked.

"Oh yeah! Everything's fine."

Amused, she laughed.

"OK," she said. "Ready to go?"

"I'm ready."

He grinned, watching her lock the door behind her, and they headed out.

Mid-July can be such a dicey time of year in the city. You've got Bastille Day to contend with (no one wants to lose their heads), and you should always beware the ides of any month (even when it's not March). Not to mention, you've got climate change and all—hey, I'm no denier. Sometimes, it can be unseasonably cool, more like late March in the evenings. Other times, you get a serious heat wave, harbinger of the long August to come. But that night, as they strolled to the restaurant, the evening air was perfect.

The restaurant he'd selected was fancier than the place he'd always taken her to. It may not have been as elegant as the upscale restaurant New Man had taken her to in London, but it was definitely better than Nick's. I know all about it because I helped him Google.

Once they'd been led to their table, without hesitation The Man pulled out The Woman's chair for her.

"Oh!" she said, surprised. "Thank you."

"You're welcome."

He cleared his throat, studying the wine list, eschewing the strong desire to just order a Budweiser. He was really trying. He hoped she was charmed by how hard he was trying this time and didn't just, you know, think he was a dork.

A waiter appeared to take their drinks order.

"Welcome," he said. "What can I get you to start?"

"How about a bottle of your best"—he looked to her, hoping to get a read, but it's impossible to mystically figure out a person's of-the-moment wine preference based on facial expression alone—"red? White?" He paused, went for it: "Champagne?"

"Champagne would be lovely," The Woman said.

"Champagne it is," The Man informed the waiter decisively.

"I'll have that right out for you," the waiter said.

"Thank you very much," The Man and The Woman said simultaneously.

As the waiter took the wine list and departed, The Man and The Woman shared a giggle at having been simultaneous together.

While another person might feel embarrassed at saying the dog had informed them of something, The Man experienced no such qualms about saying, "Gatz told me you broke up with the guy you were seeing—that, um, other writer. I'm really sorry."

The Woman swallowed but forced a smile, waving it off.

"Some things aren't meant to be," she said, clearly not wanting to discuss it any further.

All he could do was nod knowingly. Some things weren't meant to be, although he dearly hoped they'd both been wrong about them as a couple being one of those not-meant-to-be things.

"I'd much rather talk about your writing!" she segued brightly. "How's it going?"

He'd meant his sympathy about her breakup. Whatever else he might have wanted, her unhappiness wasn't on the list. But he was happy at the change in topic, because for once, he was excited to share.

"For a while there," he said, "it was really hard. Nothing I was writing was any good."

Now it was her turn to nod knowingly. She must have realized it would be hard for him, in the aftermath of their breakup, to go back to writing as though nothing was different, as if the days were the same as the ones that came before it with the only goal being to put decent words together on the page.

"In fact," The Man continued, "the first book I finished after we, um, well, it was a piece of crap."

"I'm sure it wasn't—"

"No, it really was! Utter crap, so crappy, my editor didn't even try to tell me how to fix it. We both knew it was a nonstarter."

"I'm so sorry."

"Thank you for that. But it's really OK! Because I finished a new book the other day." The Man paused, sparkling in a way he almost never did. "I'm really happy with it."

She fell backward in her seat like she'd been stunned. "But you're never happy with your work."

"I *know*!"

By this point, she must've been thinking: Who is this guy? Because whenever he'd been exclamatory in the past, it had mostly been from awkward energy, not the sheer joy he was displaying now.

"This time," he continued, still filled with wonder at the very idea that this was happening to him, that circumstances could change, that the way he felt about things could change, "I am. My editor is happy with it too. He thinks it's the best thing I've ever written."

The Woman must've felt a little of what he was feeling then, it was that contagious: the idea that things can change, that whatever you thought was set in stone could improve for the better.

"Wow," she said, admiration and respect and joy at his joy in her eyes, "I'd love to read it."

"And I'd love to have you read it."

They both settled back in comfort then. In that moment, they were truly happy, together.

Time passed as their champagne came, as their meals came: stuffed shrimp for her, because she never met a shellfish she didn't like; something he'd never heard of for him, because why not be bold for once? At least culinarily.

They laughed, they smiled, poking fun at each other, practically spilling their drinks. They were experiencing, together, the muscle memory of love.

After the waiter brought the check and the check had been duly paid, The Man stood, holding out his hand to The Woman.

"Shall we go dancing?"

She nodded, taking his hand, a wide grin spreading across her face.

"I would love to go dancing," The Woman said.

Holding hands, they walked out into the night together. There was so much hope in the air.

Chapter Thirty-Nine

Meanwhile...

In the living room, everything was still. In fact, throughout almost the whole apartment, everything was still. The only exception was the bedroom, where I'd been busily at work.

The Man may have forgotten to take the bouquet of roses he'd so carefully selected, but that didn't mean they had to go to waste. I'd taken it upon myself to dismember said bouquet with paws and claws, dousing the bed in rose petals, and was now using my teeth to make a pathway out of rose petals from the doorway to the bed.

They're gonna come home, they're gonna come home, they're gonna come home!

Not content to leave it at that, I trotted out to the living room, jumping up at the light switch over and over again until I finally got it to dim.

Mood lighting.

Chapter Forty

Same night...

People of all ages—well, upward of legal drinking age—were lining the velvet rope outside the busy venue, waiting to be let in by the bouncer guarding the door. In a city of millions and millions, there were enough people interested in dancing to golden oldies to make the place popular. Plus, people tend to be a little monkey see, monkey do about this sort of thing. They see other human beings forming a line, even if it's just one or two other humans, and they think it must be something worth queueing up for and they fall into line as well. It worked in communist Russia. It works in theme parks. How else to explain the appeal of hair-raising rides that make humans want to hurl?

But on this night, there was no waiting for The Man and The Woman. The bouncer must've sensed something special about them, because he waved them right in.

Inside, the place was youthful and upbeat, but with an older charm. The Woman immediately excused herself, and The Man sat on a tall stool at a two-top, looking around at all the dancing people having fun. He felt uncomfortable and out of place, like the collar on his shirt was tightening around his neck even though the top button had never been done up in the first place. But he instantly brightened when he saw The Woman returning to him.

The Woman sat down at the table, smiling, as the music shifted from an upbeat bop to a slow song.

The Man relaxed.

"Can I have this dance?" The Woman asked.

"It would be my honor," The Man said.

The Woman took his hand, leading him out onto the dance floor.

The Man took her in his arms, going awkward again for a bit as he fumblingly attempted to assume the lead position. She seemed a bit tense with it too.

"Are you, are you good with this?" The Man asked.

He so desperately wanted to get it right. He so desperately didn't want to offend.

"I'm good with this," The Woman said.

She looked up at him, clearly content then. And he allowed a calming, satisfied grin to escape.

As they danced, they moved closer and closer, until a nun couldn't have wedged a ruler between them if she'd tried. He no longer noticed the people all around them, dancing and on the sidelines. Eventually, he became happy simply to have her in his arms again. Eventually, she let go of whatever tension she'd still been feeling too, resting her head on his shoulder.

The two fit together. Everything had clicked back into place.

They swayed as one.

Then she lifted her head, and their eyes met and locked, their heads moving with exquisitely excruciating slowness toward each other until their mouths were just an exhale apart, and then, finally . . .

They kissed.

THEY. KISSED.

!!!

It was perfect.

Chapter Forty-One

Later...

I'd been arranging and rearranging the rose petals into various designs with my snout. What can I say? I'm a bit of a perfectionist. Plus, it's *hard* waiting for exciting things you've longed to have happen to actually happen! If I hadn't found something to do with my angsty paws, I'd have gone mad with the waiting—just mad, I tell you.

I nudged the last rose petal into place and looked over my handiwork, satisfied that I'd finally gotten the design right. The roses on the bed now formed a massive red heart. It was beautiful, if a little cheesy, and I let my tongue loll in contentment.

Suddenly, I heard a key in the lock. Ecstatic, I practically tripped over my own body as I bounded over to the front door.

I sat there panting in eagerness, waiting for the front door to open.

They're here! They're finally here . . . together!

The door clicked open, and my panting slowed, my face falling.

There stood The Man in the doorway, crestfallen and alone.

What happened???

Chapter Forty-Two

Earlier...

As the song changed again, this time shifting from slow to upbeat, a dark-haired head danced past, recognizing The Woman.

It was The Brunette.

"Hi!" The Brunette said.

Chapter Forty-Three

Later . . .

Oh no! I whimpered.
　　"Oh yes," sighed The Man.

Chapter Forty-Four

Earlier...

The Man's back was to The Brunette, but he recognized her voice, and his face fell.

"Oh, hi!" The Woman said, anxious energy infusing her voice.

"*You* like ballroom dancing?" The Brunette said, addressing her comments to The Man's back. "*I* like ballroom dancing! Maybe I'll need to sneak you away from her, you beautiful hunk of flesh, and—"

It was here that The Man turned toward The Brunette, unable to completely mask his discontent.

"Nice to see you again," he said.

The Brunette was unable to hide her shock that this was *The Man* and that the two of them were together again.

"Oh, *it's you*," she said.

The Brunette gawked at them as The Man and The Woman shared an uncomfortable moment of eye contact.

"I'll catch up with you later," The Woman said to The Brunette.

"You better."

Unable to take her eyes off them, The Brunette danced back into the crowd.

The Man and The Woman were still in their slow-dance position, even though the beat was no longer slow, and The Man stared at The Brunette, who was dancing in a hectic way by herself. Between moves,

The Brunette kept giving disapproving looks at The Man, who was finding it difficult to tear his gaze away.

A little later, the two were dancing in an upbeat fashion to upbeat music, but now The Man couldn't help but see people everywhere, and it felt like they were all staring at him. In his self-conscious state, he managed to step on The Woman's feet, more than once.

"Sorry, sorry, sorry," he said.

He felt The Woman watching him watch the room, but he couldn't stop himself. Everything seemed so uncomfortable now, and he stepped on her feet yet again.

"Sorry." He tried to laugh it off. "I, I'm not very good at this."

She pulled away for a beat, swallowed, then laughed it off as well.

"It's OK," she said. "Try this."

The Woman showed him an easy dance move, and The Man gamely copied it. Having achieved success at the easy, he felt a little more relaxed. Reacting to his more relaxed state, she eased back into it.

They danced on, happy together again.

Chapter Forty-Five

Later . . .

So that's it? The night ended well? You took her home and are gonna go out again . . .

"Let's get some fresh air," The Man said.

He opened the door, and I trotted out after him, uneasy.

Chapter Forty-Six

Earlier . . .

There'd been yet another song shift, and The Man was trying to stay in it. But he couldn't. He was too caught up in the room. He saw The Brunette, and he could've sworn she dragged her finger across her throat in a threatening manner.

He knew she hadn't really done that—who would do such a thing?—but he couldn't escape the feeling of being watched, of being judged, and he pulled back.

"Are people watching us?" he asked, anxious energy pouring out of him.

The Woman looked at him, her expression inscrutable.

"No," she said. "No one is watching us."

It was true. Everyone was in their own worlds, even The Brunette, who was doing the Charlie Brown with some impossibly tall and gorgeous man. The Man thought it might be a New York Knick. But then he realized: What would a New York Knick be doing there? His mind was going to crazy places.

The Man nodded, trying to shake it off. He moved to take her back into his arms again, but she pulled back, smiling but still inscrutable.

"Let's sit for a little while," she suggested.

Gulping, The Man nodded, allowing himself to be led off the dance floor.

She managed to snag a booth that was just being vacated and encouraged The Man to sit. Then she went over to the bar by herself to get them drinks.

The Man watched her order from the bartender. And even though he couldn't hear them, he could tell they were easily exchanging small talk. He marveled, not for the first time, at how comfortable The Woman always was out in the world.

He saw her look back at him, and this time he thought he could read her expression: wistful.

The Man slumped in the booth, knee tapping, glancing all around. He saw The Woman accept their drinks from the bartender, leaving a good tip on the bar before picking up the glasses.

She stood there for a long moment, looking across the room at The Man. He caught her glance, pushing away the anxious tells and waving at her with an eager smile.

For her part, she raised one of the glasses a little higher, as though waving back, but the accompanying smile struck him as sad.

She closed the space between them, handing him his drink and sliding into the booth across from him.

"Thanks," he said.

He took a big gulp. She took a small sip.

He smiled widely, if a little manically, at her, unable to keep his knee from commencing to bounce once more.

"So," he said, "when do you wanna get out there again? Cut the rug some more?" He waggled his eyebrows. "Maybe I could dip you this time?"

The Woman looked at him and then down at her drink, searching for the words to respond with.

The Man processed this.

Finally, she spoke.

"When we were together, before, I thought the problem was unwillingness to compromise. That if only we could compromise, we'd be OK."

"I'm really trying," he said.

"I know you are. And I love you for wanting to try."

He relaxed a little, hearing her use the word "love," particularly that she'd applied it to him. It had been a long time since he'd heard anything like it, and he'd longed to hear it again.

But then he looked into her eyes and saw that, as always, she was a step ahead of him. And then it felt like their eyes were both pleading that her next words not come out.

And still . . .

"But maybe," The Woman said, "compromise isn't always the solution."

"But I'm willing to compromise," The Man said.

He took her hand in his.

"I want to compromise for you," The Man continued. "I love you. I don't want to mess this up again."

On the verge of tears, she put her other hand on top of his.

"It's no good for me to get the things I love," she said with gentle force, "if it means you having to do the things you hate."

He knew she was right. Still . . .

"I don't have to hate it," The Man said. "I can love it! Give me a chance. I, I can do it. I will do it."

"But you do hate it," The Woman said. "You've always hated it. It's who you are."

He couldn't lie to himself anymore, and his heart sank.

"You would never ask me to change who I am to be with you," The Woman said. "I'm not going to ask you to change to be with me."

The two stared at each other across the table, knowing what they now knew. They clung to each other's hands, unwilling to let go.

This was it.

Chapter Forty-Seven

Later...

That was it?

The Man and I were up on the rooftop, something we rarely did, The Man being much more of an indoor kind of guy; except, obviously, for forays to the park, which we both love. The Man leaned his elbows on the ledge, staring out at the city. Me, I was slumped back onto my hind legs, looking up at him, crestfallen.

This is it?

How did we get back here again?

Obviously, I wasn't referring to the roof. I knew exactly how we got up there: we took the stairs. What I wanted to know was, after all that work, how did we manage to come full circle to them still being broken up? We're a Mets household, not a Yankees household, but we did have Yogi Berra for a bit, and all I gotta say is: talk about your déjà vu all over again!

Holding back tears, The Man looked down at me, his little buddy.

"That was it," The Man said.

We stared at each other then, feeling each other's pain, existing together, just taking it all in. The Man turned his attention back to the city.

"You know, Gatz," The Man said, "I just want her to be happy." He paused. "Even if it's not with me."

How could you say that? You two are meant to be together!

"I know what you're thinking."

Clearly.

The Man looked down at me again, his brow furrowed, like he was working something out for the first time.

"When you love someone, you should want what's best for them. Not what's best for them in relation to you."

He let that sink in for a moment, for him as well as for me.

"You should want them to be happy in whatever form it takes. And for her, for *both* of us . . . that's not with each other."

I was heartbroken. I had no words.

But there was one detail that was puzzling me.

This was Friday night, the weekend, meaning I was supposed to be with her.

Once more, The Man did his mind-reading thing. For a guy who doesn't always pick up on social cues, he can be amazingly intuitive. At least with me.

"She and I agreed," he said, "that it'd be less disruptive, for everybody, if she came for you tomorrow morning instead of tonight."

Gotcha.

The Man yawned, rubbing at his eyes.

"That took a lot out of me," he said. "Let's go to bed."

Woefully, I nodded, trotting behind him inside and back to our apartment.

Once there, he rubbed my ears, kissing me on the forehead.

"I love you, Gatz," he said.

Then he disappeared into the bedroom.

Almost immediately, I heard him wonder aloud, "Where did all these rose petals come from?"

Normally, I would've followed him in there and done my best to communicate an answer to his question.

But these weren't normal times, and I was too caught up in my own thoughts.

How could I have been so wrong about everything? They weren't . . . happy together?

A scene from the past played out in my head from back during the holidays, their third and last holiday season together. The tree had been haphazardly half-decorated. The Hanukkah candles had gone unlit. The two had tried to feign enthusiasm, probably for my sake, but neither of them had been invested in the process anymore.

Was it possible that I'd been wrong all these years? Was it possible that The Man and The Woman had mistaken, and I had mistaken, their mutual intense love for me for love for each other? Of course, love had been there, but maybe they should have always been just friends, the *best* of friends, but it was never really True Love.

I sank into the couch, mulling it all over, The Man's words coming back to me.

When you love someone, you should want what's best for them. Not what's best for them in relation to you . . . What's best for them . . .

My wheels were turning.

And oh, what wheels they were!

I remembered The Woman telling her work friends about meeting New Man for the first time at the London Book Fair. I pictured what that must've been like: a smile escaping his face as he looked down at her, the same smile—but with her lips and teeth, of course—escaping hers as she looked up at him.

I pictured them later, when they'd gone out to the fancy restaurant together, laughing over their first meal.

I pictured them each reaching for a bottle of wine at the same time during Book Club, their fingers lingering. They couldn't help but blush and smile.

I pictured the two of them splashing around in the pool at her parents' place in the Hamptons, having a fun time. Probably not editing.

Finally, I recalled that night at New Man's apartment. I'd been so caught up in the view, I hadn't taken in their reflection in the window, hadn't seen what was really going on. But as I closed my eyes now, casting my mind back to picture it all, I could suddenly see New Man and The Woman slow-dancing in the reflection. They were happy and content, and taking this all in now, I was happy and content for them to be so.

I was touched by these memories.

He IS what's best for her. He IS what's good for her. But I—

I was filled with shame then, recalling my own bad behavior.

I pictured myself nastily barking at New Man in her kitchen, completely unprovoked. I pictured myself glaring at New Man during the dinner on the lawn at her family's place in the Hamptons, prompting him to put down his burger. I pictured myself in New Man's kitchen, lunging at New Man to knock the box with the ring in it out of his hand, causing him to yell at me that I was stupid—which, I now saw, I was—and The Woman recoiling from him.

I'd been proud of myself in the moment, but now?

I was horrified at my own actions.

I . . . I'm making her unhappy.

Of all the things I'd ever intended to do in my life, that had never been one of them.

I trotted into the bedroom to check on The Man.

The Man was sacked out under the covers, and I watched him from the doorway. I can usually tell when his sleep is troubled, but curiously, he seemed to be sleeping just fine.

Maybe I can't make both of them happy, I thought. *Maybe I can't make them be happy together. But I know how to make at least one of them happy.*

Chapter Forty-Eight

The next day...

I'd have thought that, given what had gone on between them the night before, things would be more awkward than ever when The Woman came to get me that morning. But sometimes, humans can surprise you.

They chatted easily in the doorway, easier with each other than they'd been since before their breakup. He even offered her a cup of coffee. She even accepted. They even shared a laugh over The Brunette's "dancing skills." When two people can share a laugh together, it's always a good sign.

I'm not going to say it was perfect. You could tell there was an undercurrent of sadness still, but they were OK enough. They were OK with each other. And, in time, I thought they'd be even more than OK. With a love as deep as they'd shared and with their shared love of me, how could they not be friends? I might have been wrong about a thing or two recently, but this was one thing I knew for certain.

We couldn't tarry there forever, though, could we? I mean, the whole point of joint custody was for me to spend weekends with her. Since it was Saturday—glorious Saturday!—we soon found ourselves at her place.

She'd stopped for groceries on the way, and I waited somewhat impatiently for her to put them away. At last, she said, "OK, buddy, is there anything special you want to do today?"

The Woman turned to find me with the leash in my mouth, thumping my tail incessantly.

I was ready to go out.

Oh boy, was I ready.

Chapter Forty-Nine

The same day...

Out on the sidewalk, the sun was shining. It was a beautiful day.

"It's such a gorgeous day today," The Woman said, "isn't it?"

Usually, I keep pace with her. But this time, I pulled her along, trotting at a brisk pace.

"Do you have somewhere you need to be?" she asked, sounding amused.

But I had no time for chatter.

When we reached the end of the block, she started to turn left. Nope. I pulled her straight.

"OK, bud," she said. "We can play it your way."

At every block corner, I pulled her in the opposite direction of where she was attempting to go. With great determination, I dragged her all over town. Perhaps she thought me mad. But if I was mad, it was only north by northwest. Because I had a purpose and a direction. Steadily, inexorably, I was leading her uptown.

I'll admit, occasionally I got distracted, stopping to bark loudly at a truck or sniff at a falafel cart before remembering I was a canine with a mission. But, mostly, I was inexorable.

"Aren't you getting tired?" she said at one point. "Let's head back."

I pulled her forward again, harder.

She shrugged.

Eventually, the buildings around us must've begun to look very familiar to her. We had arrived in New Man's neighborhood.

"Gatz, let's turn back," she said, unsettled.

I hated to unsettle her, but I knew what I was doing. I know I'd thought that before (more than once), and I'd been wrong before (more than once), but this time I was right. (I was almost sure of it.)

Please be right, please be right, please be right.

Ignoring that she was unsettled, I plowed on. Onward and upward.

"Gatz, there are treats for you at home. Let's go back."

Nope.

"Gatz." I could hear the anxiety in her voice.

Suddenly, I stopped in my tracks, parking myself on the sidewalk, and looked up. She looked up too. New Man's apartment loomed above us.

"Gatz, what are you doing?"

She stared at me. I stared back at her.

"Gatz, let's go."

No matter how much I might've hated to disobey her—and I did, border collies being pretty much the most obedient breed in the world—I refused to budge.

I bored my eyes into hers.

She groaned.

"Gatz, it's nearly ten. He's going to be back from his morning jog any minute now. *Let's go.*"

I cemented my butt to the concrete. I may weigh only twenty-two pounds, but I can be a deadweight whenever I want to.

"Gatz, what are you doing?" she pleaded with me.

Still not budging.

She stared at me, heartbroken.

Then came the sound of footsteps approaching, and reluctantly, she turned her head toward those footsteps.

It was New Man, sweaty and catching his breath. I had to admit that even post-workout, he was gorgeous.

If she looked heartbroken to see him, he looked equally heart-broken to see her.

"Hi," he said.

"Hi," she said.

Well, at least it was a start.

But a start wasn't good enough!

I pulled away from The Woman, her grip on the leash loosening due to her distracted state, and bounded toward New Man.

He flinched, understandably scared—given his past experience with that stupid English mastiff and the fact I was bounding at him—but I merely jumped up and down at his feet, joyfully, giving him loving licks with each joyful jump.

It was clear that New Man could hardly believe it and that The Woman could hardly believe it either.

I wagged my tail, panting happily, grinning up at New Man, rubbing my head against his leg to let him know I finally meant him well.

The initial shock subsiding, New Man began to laugh, in awe, while The Woman looked on in wonder.

New Man leaned down, cautiously, holding a tentative hand above my head, not quite making contact with me.

"Is it OK if I—" he started to say.

In answer, I moved my head upward to meet New Man's hand, and New Man began to rub me behind my ears, tentatively at first but then with growing confidence.

"But . . . he hated me," New Man said. "What changed?"

"I don't know," The Woman said, as stunned as he was. "He brought me here."

New Man couldn't contain himself. He looked overcome with a happiness he could barely let himself feel as he smiled at me.

"Do you . . . want us to be together, Gatz?" The Woman asked.

I became more eager, licking New Man more and more. Then I lay on my back just as I had done with The Woman so many times before, offering up my belly for a rub—vulnerable, but ready for love.

"I think he does!" New Man said.

Now, New Man was really getting into it, rubbing me all over.

"Who's a good dog?" he said. "Who's a good dog?"

I pulled back, slightly grossed out. Sorry, but that question can be annoying.

We'll have to work on that.

New Man, embarrassed, nodded back.

Then the two of them looked at each other: affirmation at what was happening. Real affection. Love.

New Man stood upright, looked to The Woman. They were both ecstatic as they rapidly closed the space between them, holding on to each other and kissing.

I watched, touched and happy for them.

They pulled apart, laughing, nearly crying, so happy to be back together.

I got it.

I was nearly crying myself.

And that . . . that was True Love.

The two couldn't take their eyes off of each other, but they did when I bounded over, looping myself through their legs.

New Man and The Woman laughed, leaning down to pet me together.

Now all I had to do was find True Love for The Man.

Chapter Fifty

One month later...

It was another sunny day in the city. Beautiful! Considering it was August, it was as close to perfection as we were ever going to get.

The 92nd Street Y was filled to capacity, everyone in the space eager. On the stage, there were two comfortable chairs, empty and slightly angled toward each other, with a small table for water bottles and whatnot between them and a speaker's podium to one side.

I was to the right of the stage, looping myself around the legs of New Man and The Woman, who was there because one of her authors was featured in the event, which was called "Tell Us About Your Process."

I looked up at The Woman and New Man in awe. They were so in love.

"Your brother called today," New Man said.

I briefly wondered if he meant Tall or Short. But then I figured it had to be Tall. Tall was the only one who'd call New Man out of the blue like that. Well, Short might call if it was about food.

"Yes?" The Woman said. "What did he say?"

"He said he wanted your help looking for his finger?" New Man said, perplexed.

"Oh my god."

"Do you know what that could be about?"

"Ignore that," The Woman said, tucking her hair behind one ear.

When she moved her hand, I could see the big honking diamond sparkle on her ring finger. Big as it was, however, it managed to not be tacky or gaudy. New Man is like that: rich but still with great taste and a lot of class.

I glanced over at the other side of the stage, where The Man stood with his editor, waiting to go on. I was sure The Man would be a bundle of nerves right around now, and I trotted over to the left to see if I could lend a helping paw. What can I say? Most people have heard of support dogs, but I'm a *supportive* dog.

"Do you think anyone would notice if I took off now?" The Man asked.

The Editor glared, looking around the room. "Oh, not at all," he said with an eye roll, "you'd slip right out."

"I feel like a sausage." He tugged at his collar as if it was growing tight, but of course it wasn't. He was in his usual uniform of flannel shirt opened over white T-shirt and jeans plus backward Mets ball cap. "I'm sausaged in here."

"Relax," The Editor said. "It's going to be fine. You're not even here to talk up a specific book. All they want to hear about is your writing process."

"OK." Deep breath. "OK."

"You've got this," The Editor said.

As he said this supportive thing, I saw another man approach them, immediately taking hold of The Editor's hand. I realized this must be The Editor's husband, whom he'd previously referred to as "the love of my life," and I saw that this was true.

Once upon a time, and for a very long time, I'd detested The Editor. But I'd softened when I heard him tell The Man that he was "the best writer I know."

It occurred to me then that, just like I'd been wrong about New Man from the start, perhaps I'd been wrong about The Editor from the start too. Maybe he'd never been the bad guy I thought him to be.

Maybe he just wanted to help The Man be the best writer he could be, editing him in the best way he knew how. So, his style might have been different than that of The Woman, but his editorial heart was in the right place.

But I still wasn't going to let him rank on us for only keeping beer in the fridge.

I approached another dog to sniff butt back over on The Woman's side of the stage, and as I did so, I saw a woman approach her. Based on her appearance and the description I'd heard of her once, I immediately knew who she was: The Woman's Author, the one she'd had with her when she did the panel at the London Book Fair. Hispanic female, flannel shirt open over a tank top and jeans, pigtailed hair beneath baseball cap, which she wore backward.

The Woman's Author looked as nervous as The Man, so it didn't surprise me to see The Woman embrace her warmly.

"Are you nervous?" The Woman asked.

Obvious question, perhaps. But you can't begin to solve a problem until you acknowledge it.

"Do you see how many people there are here?" The Woman's Author asked. "Oh my god, this is just awful."

"It's going to be fine," The Woman said reassuringly. "Breathe."

"What if they can hear me when I'm breathing up there?"

"No one's going to—"

"I bet they can smell my fear."

"You're going to be great. Hey." She placed her hands on her author's arms, looked her steadily in the eye. "You're going to be great. I promise."

The Woman's Author nodded along, visibly trying to shake off her nerves.

They hugged again, and as they hugged, I craned my neck to see if I could catch a gander at the logo on The Woman's Author's ball cap, if there was one. Huh. Just as I suspected, it was the Mets.

The Woman's Author took a deep breath. Squinting to peer at the other side of the stage, I saw The Man take a deep breath at the same time.

Just then, New Man leaned down to whisper in my ear, "Wanna sit down, bud? I think they're almost ready to start."

I panted happily with my tongue out. In the past month, we'd grown very comfortable together.

New Man and The Woman took their seats, which were reserved and in the front row center, me lounging at their feet. As we sat there, New Man petted me, and it occurred to me for the first time: the guy now loved me, and not just to make her happy. He loved me for myself.

I watched The Woman's Author and The Man walk across the stage toward each other from opposite sides, each not really taking in the other, so caught up were they in their individual awkward nervousness. They took their seats, trying to get settled, as stagehands moved around them setting up mics.

Side by side, the visual was striking.

The Woman's Author and The Man, both dressed in their flannels, both with their ball caps on backward. *Mets* ball caps.

They stared forward, still not seeing each other.

She rested her left ankle on her right knee. He rested his left ankle on his right knee.

She bounced her right knee. He bounced his right knee.

The gears turned in my head.

Oh my god.

"Oh my god!!!"

Wait. Had I said that out loud?

No, I saw with some measure of relief, because if I could suddenly talk too, that might be too much even for me. The speaker had been The Redhead, who was now rushing toward The Woman. The Redhead was accompanied by their other two work friends.

"Hi!" The Woman said, hugging them all at once. "I'm so glad you could make it!"

"For a discussion on the author's gaze on projection and intersectional rights in the book industry?" The Blonde asked. Not waiting for an answer, which was just as well since she'd have been disappointed to learn that was *not* the topic, she added, "Wouldn't miss it!"

"I had to cancel my goat's acupuncture appointment for this," The Brunette said. "I just hope it's worth it."

Sure, the work friends were interesting if odd, but I couldn't take my eyes off The Woman's Author and The Man up on the stage.

I mean, look at them.

The Woman's Author adjusted her chair nervously. The Man adjusted his chair nervously.

She adjusted her mic. He adjusted his mic.

She leaned on her left palm. He leaned on his left palm.

It was like watching the old Harpo Marx / Lucille Ball routine.

She's antisocial, she doesn't care about fashion, she's perfect! Does anyone else see what I'm seeing?

Simultaneously, The Woman's Author and The Man took big, laborious breaths and let them out.

They're perfect for each other!

The Woman took her seat beside us and looked up at the stage, content. The Man met her gaze, and they gave each other a smile, completely devoid of sadness, and a nod. They were OK together now.

I beat my tail, happy to see how OK they were.

The Woman looked at New Man, and it was obvious to me how in love they both were with each other. It wasn't really the place for PDA, but if it were, I'd bet he'd wrap his arms around her and give her a big kiss. And me, I'd be happy for them. I was happy for them.

On the stage, The Woman's Author and The Man cleared their throats in unison. At the sounds, they looked over at each other for the first time, wonder and then recognition dawning in their eyes:

kindred spirits. Despite the nerves they'd both been visibly feeling just a second ago, now they were all big smiles. At each other.

If I had to give a label to what I was witnessing—and who among us is above the desire to label?—I'd have to say it was love at first sight, pure and simple.

Maybe we should all just start calling her New Woman now?

And if they needed any nudges in the right direction? I'd make sure they got there. Having retired from my days as a wingdog, I was now a matchmaker extraordinaire. And forget about meaning*less*. From this day forward, I was going to be all about the meaning*ful*.

"Can I have everyone's attention?" a man called from behind the podium.

The crowd began to settle, and even though it wasn't a musical event, taking in the faces of The Woman, New Man, The Man, and New Woman—all looking so happy—a song instantly began playing in my mind:

You know the song, and if you don't, Google and YouTube are your friends.

"Just the Way You Are," by Bruno Mars, of course.

There's a Bruno Mars song for everything.

Sometimes, you don't get the happily ever after you hoped for and worked for, or even thought you'd get, but that's OK. Just so long as everyone winds up happy.

It's all about the happy ending.

Acknowledgments

Going through the writing and publishing process at any time comes with its challenges, but the events of 2020 really called on next-level efforts, so we would both like to thank:

Pamela Harty, for her great friendship and for always believing in us, and everyone else at The Knight Agency;

Cindy Hwang, for wanting our book; Angela Kim, for holding our hands at all the stages; Marianne Aguiar, for superior copyediting; Sarah Oberrender, for her gorgeous cover design; Jennifer Myers, for a production schedule that didn't miss a beat; Fareeda Bullert, for marketing; the sales team and everyone else at Penguin Random House who has worked so hard, going above and beyond to bring our book to you; booksellers, librarians, reviewers, and readers everywhere.

Lauren would like to thank: Lauren Catherine, Bob Gulian, Andrea Schicke Hirsch, Greg Logsted, Rob Mayette, and Krissi Petersen Schoonover, all of whom have contributed their talent and support to the Crow's Nest Writers Group over the years; my extended family and friends; my husband, Greg, for life, love, and Jackie; Jackie, for everything.

Jackie would like to thank: my parents, for a love and support that could move mountains and for getting me where I am today. To Ben, Ariel, Natura, Emma, Hana, Charlotte, Laura, Elise, who have made my college experience what it is, and left an impression on my life that is endless. To Erin Clarke for her photography and friendship. And finally, to Planes—may you fly high and not crash too many times on your way.

Finally, from both of us again: We would like to thank you, whoever you are, holding this book right now.

Read on for a special glimpse at the sequel to

Joint Custody

Prologue

A famous Russian writer once said that "Happy families are all alike; every unhappy family is unhappy in its own way." Well, I don't know what the Russian word is for "bollocks," but since The Woman is English, I'm well versed in what the English word is and it's: bollocks.

Just like the Jane Austen line—"It is a truth universally acknowledged, that a single man in possession of a good fortune, must be in want of a wife"—is not universal at all, and is only true of the specific world Austen created, the same is true of Leo Tolstoy's diss on happy families. It is true in his world. But in *the* world, the one I inhabit, happy families are not all alike. Indeed, just like unhappy families, they are infinite in their variety.

I happen to know this for a fact because I happen to come from a happy family; two, actually—the one I inhabit with The Man (who, OK, isn't always a bundle of joy and occasionally suffers from depression, but we are happy together) and the one I inhabit with The Woman and New Man.

But just because it's a happy world we've made for ourselves, it doesn't mean we're a bunch of giddily mindless twits. It doesn't mean we don't have our share of troubles, conflicts, and heartaches.

Yeah, about those . . .

But maybe I should back up for a minute. If this is the first time for a reader encountering me, that reader would be justified in asking: Who's telling this story? Who's quoting Tolstoy and Austen at the reader right off the bat?

The answer: me. Gatz. A dog. Black and white. Border collie. If I were a cat, I would be a fat cat, but since I'm not, my twenty-two pounds makes me a lean, mean fighting machine. Ah, I'm just funnin' ya. I'm not a fighter! I'm a lover!

Now here's where some might begin to object: The *dog* is telling the story? To which I would point out that all good narratives require the willing suspension of disbelief. So I would heartily encourage all who enter here to just be willing and suspend.

Having introduced myself, I'm going to further take this opportunity to bring everyone up to speed.

Once upon a time, I was rescued from a shelter by The Man, a thirtysomething schlub with an apartment in Brooklyn and a career as a literary novelist. On the day he rescued me, while walking home, we encountered The Woman: British, Black, and beautiful, making her a trifecta in the B department. She was an editor in the city. As far as I was concerned, it was love for all of us at first sight, and indeed love and cohabitation soon followed. That state of bliss lasted for a while, but over time their differences got the best of them—he's an introvert, she's an extrovert, they were "oil-and-watering" each other—and she moved out.

There ensued a period in which I did everything in my doggy power, including a suicidal run-in with a box of Valentine's Day chocolates, to bring them back together. But all my efforts were to no avail once The Woman met New Man, a bestselling novelist and a dead ringer for Henry Golding. How could The Man, how could *any* man compete with that? Not to mention, New Man was an extrovert too, who loved doing all the things The Man hated to do, so they had the stuff-in-common thing going for them as a couple too. Feh.

I wanted to hate the guy—for a long time I *did* hate the guy—and I certainly let him know it. But after a long journey of pushing him away and a failed reconciliation between The Man and The Woman, I had an epiphany if you will: When you love someone, you should want what's best for them, not what's best for them in relation to you.

Cliché, it may be, but I read the writing on the wall, and that writing told me that New Man was right for The Woman in ways that The Man never had been and never could be, not without at least one person winding up miserable. The Man and The Woman had come together over their shared love of me. The Woman and New Man, however? They fell in love with each other.

So, here's where we left off the last time. It was August. The Woman and New Man had recently become engaged and were in the audience at an author event at the 92nd Street Y. On the panel were The Man and one other person, one of The Woman's authors, who I'd previously thought of simply that way. But a lightbulb went on over my head when I noticed that the author, Hispanic and cute in her braids, was a female version of The Man, right down to her backward Mets baseball cap and her clear antipathy for anything social. Could this person actually be New Woman? Could these two find love in the same way The Woman and New Man had? Could there be romantic hope for The Man yet?

I hope we're all on the same page now. Well, obviously we are, since I'm writing it and you're reading it.

Now that that's been established, we can turn that page together . . .

Chapter One

September

•

Most people reckon the New Year begins on January 1, but I favor September. Maybe it's the school-year thing. Sure, I've never been to school myself, not even obedience school—*why would I ever need such a thing?*—but it is when all the kids traditionally go back. It's also the month Rosh Hashanah falls, the Jewish New Year, and while The Man is currently nonpracticing, I like to keep abreast of all the major holidays. You never know what could happen; you never know when things might suddenly change; you never know when good ol' Gatz might be called upon to don a yarmulke. I bet I'd wear one with elan.

So, September: a time for new beginnings, a season of renewal, change in the air.

What better time for The Woman to finally move in with New Man?

By this point, they'd been engaged for several weeks already. And while some might wonder why they didn't move in together immediately upon their engagement, I didn't. Hey, it's enough for me to be able to figure out all the general vagaries of human behavior, I don't need to get lost in the weeds of every little detail. If I thought about it at all, I probably figured the delay had to do with deciding what to do about her own place, which her parents actually owned, or maybe she didn't want to rush-rush everything like she'd done when she first met The Man; you know, maybe she was doing the live-and-learn thing.

Anyway, Moving Day had arrived!

I confess to being a bit anxious about it myself. Not everyone realizes this, but moving from one domicile to another is a Top Ten item for humans when it comes to anxiety. And while I try to be as zen as possible about most things, I had my concerns.

As anxious-making as it can be to move in general, it's got to be exponential when you're moving into someone else's space. If the place is new for everyone then it's equally new for everyone. But if one of the people already lives there, it's not equal: it's *their space*! Similarly, if you're the person whose space it already is, then when someone else moves into it—bringing along her dog, say—it wouldn't be surprising if that person experienced some sense of invasion, like: Hey, you're in *my space*!

So, yeah, I had my anxieties about it. And on some level, I must have assumed that they wouldn't want me around on Moving Day, even though it occurred on the weekend, my normal time to be with The Woman, that and most holidays as per her joint-custody agreement with The Man. I figured that it might be a bit of a nuisance, having a dog underfoot when you're trying to figure out if the credenza should stay where it's always been or if maybe it would work better against another wall.

New Man, however, was having none of it.

"Of course, Gatz will be with us on Moving Day," he said, flashing his beautiful, charming, sweet smile at The Woman when she suggested that maybe it would be more convenient if she and The Man flipped their days with me that week. "Who else is going to tell me where to put my credenza?"

This guy, man. He was growing on me by the second.

New Man lives in the penthouse of a high rise—actually has a special key to use in the elevator—and it's already decorated to perfection. With the exception of the mirrored bathroom floor—which I happen to like, but I get that others might find tacky—everything is perfectly appointed, every design decision exuding understated elegance. Because when you have a view like New Man's—a floor-to-ceiling giant pane of glass spanning one entire wall and offering a view of the city that I doubt could be rivaled anywhere else *in* the city—you don't need to gild the lily with a whole bunch of tacky gold *this* and tacky gold *that*.

Not that any of The Woman's possessions are tacky. She herself is taste personified, which probably should've given me pause in her previous relationship with The Man, who is anything but. I guess it never had, though, until they broke up, because I happen to love the schlub myself, just as he is.

So, no, I hadn't worried that her things would clash with New Man's, but I had worried about the logistics of things. When she'd moved in with The Man, he'd first made space in the closet, made space in the bathroom, and, most important of all, made space in his bookshelves. The Man, though, wasn't much of a nester. Except for his collection of books and a few select articles of clothing, he wasn't married to any material objects. It didn't matter. But all the items of New Man's were so well chosen, so well placed, how could he not object to us bringing along our own stuff and messing with his fêng shui?

The Woman and I took the elevator up to the penthouse apartment using her own new special key. The Woman carrying a box in her arms, and me carrying some toys in my jaw. She grinned down at me, and I looked up at her (my eyes glistening at her beauty, I'm sure).

"Are you ready, Gatz?" she asked me.

That was The Woman all over. She always thought of me. She always thought of us all.

I dropped my toys and barked my approval.

When we arrived, me trotting in more anxious still, it soon became apparent that New Man hadn't done anything in advance of our coming.

Did he not know what day it was?

"I kept thinking I should be doing something," he said, running a hand through his gloriously thick black hair. "I should be making room, clearing a shelf in the bookcase, adding a hook for your coffee mug next to mine even though I don't hang my mugs on hooks, moving all my clothes over to one side of the closet. But then I thought, why do that?"

Because it's the polite thing to do?

"That would be going about it all wrong."

It would be?

And, may I add here that The Woman and I shared a perplexed look at this turn of events. Perhaps she too had been experiencing some advance anxiety over an anticipated transitional awkwardness?

"From the looks on your faces," New Man said, "I can tell I'm expressing myself wrong."

Clearly.

And him a writer—HAH!

"If I'd done that," New Man said, trying again, "then you'd always feel, both you and Gatz, like 'OK, then, this is my small space here—my small place in the closet, etcetera—within his much larger space.' Do you see how wrong that would be?"

I was beginning to. From the growing curiosity in her eyes, I could tell The Woman was beginning to see it too.

"I want it all, everything here and every inch of it," New Man said, spreading his arms wide, "to be *our* space—all three of ours, whenever Gatz is here."

"Meaning?" The Woman said.

"Put your stuff wherever you want it, move anything you want to move, get rid of anything you hate. Like, for example, the credenza. Gatz, what do you think? Is it right where it is, should we move it, or even get rid of it entirely?"

I tilted my head to one side to better regard the piece of furniture in question. Eh, I had no quarrel with the credenza.

While I was doing that, The Woman closed the space between her and New Man, landing a passionate kiss on his lips. When the two pulled away, a surprised blush escaped across his face. "What was that for?"

"For being you." She smiled, holding him close in her arms. "For wanting it all to be ours. And for making me feel instantly like it all is."

I thumped my tail enthusiastically and let out a happy bark so they'd both know that I felt the same.

Immediately, all my anxiety left me. What had I been so worried about?

That's the funny thing I've learned about anxiety, worry, and a whole host of negative emotions: Unless feeling it is going to make you do something to change your behavior in a positive way, what good does it do? What purpose does it serve? Nothing whatsoever, except to make the person experiencing it feel bad. And, worst of all, lots of times you feel these things in advance, and then the thing you were advance-anxious about never comes to pass, and all your anxiety is for naught. Yeah, I know all this, on an intellectual level. But on an emotional level? In the moment, I do tend to forget.

"So," New Man said, "what do you want to change first?"

"Nothing," The Woman said, laughing. I guess all the anxiety had left her too. "We can do whatever needs doing later. But what I'd really like right now is . . ."

Oh, please say dinner! Please say dinner! Please say dinner!

". . . dinner," she finished.

YES!

So that's what we did. We ordered takeout, glorious takeout, and while we waited for it to arrive, The Woman did make one tiny design change to New Man's penthouse; I mean, *their* penthouse. Or, better yet, *our* penthouse.

On my first-ever visit there, I'd noticed that in the hallway leading to the master bedroom, New Man had family photos on the wall; I'd been particularly struck by the one of what I assumed to be his younger sister. Now, The Woman dug out her own framed family photos. New Man found her a hammer and some nails, and beside his family photos, she hung pictures of her parents; her brothers, Tall (the nosy one) and Short (the food-obsessed one), with their own spouses and kids; and me.

Now family photos stretched down the hallway wall as far as my eye could see.

New Man put his arm around The Woman's shoulders. She put her arm around his waist. They tilted their heads together as they looked at the wall.

"Ours," they said at the same time, exhaling happy sighs.

My heart was full to bursting.

Here's the thing about happy families: they can't exist without happy people, and my family was full of them. We had happy people who ate takeout together, and happy people who talked books together, and happy people who shared joint custody of the ol' Gatzer together. What else could one want?

So suck it, Tolstoy. Happy people are infinite in their variety, and fascinating, and fairly devoid of conflict. I don't know about you, but I am living a pretty high life over here. Was there anyone who did happy families better than we did?

I must confess, I was feeling pret-ty smug about that fact.

And, as great as I felt then, I felt even better when the doorman called up to say our takeout had arrived.

And that was topped when New Man placed a carton of moo shu chicken on a china plate, but leaving the food in the carton, just the way I like it, and all for me.

I figured maybe New Man would want them to eat their first meal as cohabitants at the dining room table. But he had other plans.

"I was thinking," he suggested, "movie marathon?"

What could be better? I thought, as he brought the food into the TV room, where the biggest home entertainment system I'd ever seen lived, with a curved screen and everything.

I'll tell you what could be better—he let *me* pick out the movies!

It was a dog-movie marathon from start to finish, all the greatest hits: *Benji, Beethoven, The Incredible Journey,* although there is also a cat in that last one. But for once, I didn't mind. In fact, the only time I objected was when New Man tried to offer me a Lassie movie. Color me not a fan. That dog just sets the bar too high. Plus, I'm a city dog. When am I ever going to get a chance to save Timmy from the well? It's just an impossible standard to measure up to.

But the standard of happy people?

We were better than all the people.

We *won* at being people.

Lauren Baratz-Logsted is the author of forty books for adults, teens, and children, including the Sisters 8 series for young readers, which she created with her husband, Greg Logsted, and their daughter, Jackie. Her books have been published in fifteen countries. She has yet to meet a jigsaw puzzle that could defeat her. Lauren lives with her family in Connecticut where, surprisingly, she has a cat.

Jackie Logsted is a college student studying film, screenwriting, and American Studies, training to write and direct movies. She created the Sisters 8 series with her mother and father, and had a short story published in *Ink Stains*, vol. 7. She knows her cat would be jealous to find out she wrote a book about a dog, so she chooses not to tell him. At college, she runs into many dogs, and never condescendingly calls them "buddy."